THE PORTANCE DYNASTY - BOOK ONE
the making of a prince

a story by

Bruce Edward Butler

THE PORTANCE DYNASTY
BOOK ONE
THE MAKING OF A PRINCE

Bruce Edward Butler
Website: bruceedwardbutler.com
E-mail: author@bruceedwardbutler.com

Copyright © 2007 by Bruce E. Butler

No part of this book may be reproduced or transmitted in any form or by any means, electronic or mechanical, including photocopying, recording, or by any information storage and retrieval system, without permission in writing from the copyright holder.

ACKNOWLEDGMENTS

Thanks, Karin. Your help and
support made this possible.

Test readings by
Glenda Cox
Clara Clark
Rose Mateace

Unbridled enthusiasm supplied by
Glenda Cox
Clara Clark
Rose Mateace.

Special thanks to Barbara Fandrich
For final editing and encouraging words
bjfandrich@hotmail.com

Special appreciation to the men and women of Inverness Jail who listened and approved of this story for ten years before it was put in writing.

CONTENTS

1. THE UNTHINKABLE — 1
2. SABOTHENIA — 9
3. OMENS AND PORTENTS — 15
4. THE GRIM REALITY — 23
5. ALL THE KING'S HORSES — 29
6. THE ROOT OF THE TREE — 41
7. HOPE DEFERRED — 47
8. SUBSTANCE OF THINGS HOPED FOR — 53
9. THE BEST LAID PLANS — 63
10. THE FINAL TEST — 71
11. CONFESSION — 77
12. PAINFUL PIECES — 85
13. THE CORONATION — 91

Chapter 1
THE UNTHINKABLE

At the Royal Mansion, the king and queen had a rather large household staff to see to all their needs. A governess took care of baby Prince Renaldo for a good part of each day. His life remained tranquil regardless of the swarm of circumstances surrounding his parents. His mother was usually with him by early afternoon and his father by dinnertime. The mornings were rather leisurely for the governess and the baby. Often around ten o'clock, in the spring, they could be seen strolling through the royal grounds. At that time, the child was one year old and able to enjoy the fresh air and the warmth of the morning sun.

Our story begins on one such morning stroll. It was a quintessential spring day in 1970, with all of the necessary elements: the golden warming rays of sun, birds chattering and singing, morning mist rising from the dew-covered foliage and lawns, and new life springing, budding and blossoming everywhere. It was the kind of day you might let your guard down and breathe in life as if the world will go on forever.

Yet on that very day, in that very setting, an event occurred which rocked the world and changed the lives of all the people of this small nation forever. Prince Renaldo's governess was found unconscious in the bushes. The security personnel had become alarmed by a ten-minute delay in the end of the morning stroll. When they found her, it was determined she had been drugged; probably with an inhaled anesthetic. The baby's stroller was also found hidden in the shrubbery. The prince, however, was nowhere to be found. The baby was missing.

Having recently returned from vacation and sporting fresh suntans, the king and queen were sitting for a photo session. That is when an obviously panicked aide rushed in and pulled the king aside. Abject terror is the only way to describe the king's reaction, and he tried to calm himself before he informed Pristina. They held each other tightly as they were rushed from the palace to the mansion and arrived shortly after the first policemen reached the scene. A complete search of the entire mansion and grounds had commenced, and more policemen joined in as they arrived. Standing at the spot of the abduction, the queen collapsed and had to be carried inside and revived. Throngs of law enforcement personnel converged on the Royal Estate. The governess, suffering from neck strain and a severe headache, was not able to shed any more light on the event. She could only remember being grabbed from behind and then everything going black.

Victor Swortha, Lord of the National Police Force, arrived to take charge of the search and investigation. Swortha was a highly trained professional. He was an advanced trainer for Interpol and respected in international circles for his innovative techniques and expertise. An all-points bulletin was issued throughout the nation, briefing law enforcement personnel of the kidnapping. The borders, airports and train stations were immediately shut down. He ordered the crime scene cleared and cordoned off. Forensic science was by no means as developed in 1970 as in present day, but crime scene investigation was, at that time, a very important part of detective work. Search of the grounds and the estate was soon completed without any sign of the missing prince.

Swortha assembled all of the Royal Mansion staff and had his detectives question each of them. Soon, it was early afternoon and there were still no clues revealing what had happened to the prince, other than the fact that he was missing. Intense questioning of the staff provided no leads. They had an approximate time of the abduction set at 10:12 a.m. Shortly, an observant officer came forth with evidence that someone had scaled a wall not far from the scene of the crime. Though some shoe marks could be clearly seen on the masonry perimeter wall, the thick sod on both sides did not allow any footprint impressions. Further investigation revealed no fingerprints or other evidence.

Several newspaper people had gathered outside the Royal Estate and were requesting a briefing. Swortha, after conferring with the king, walked out to the front gate and stepped into the street to face them. He presented the facts that were known.

Swortha: "Today, at approximately 10:12 a.m., Prince Renaldo was abducted from the Royal Estate. Your cooperation in getting the word out and making the general public aware of the circumstances would be much appreciated. Someone, somewhere in the country, may have seen something unusual that could help the investigation."

Unidentified newsperson: "How are the king and the queen dealing with the crisis?"

Swortha: "As you might expect, they are under tremendous duress at the moment and are in seclusion."

Unidentified newsperson: "Has there been a ransom note or contact from the abductors?"

Swortha: "There has been no contact or note. We have a contact phone number that we are asking you to make public. It is 554-7721. This number is for the abductors only, and we are asking the citizens with information to contact the police department."

At that time, I pulled up with my cameraman in our van from National Television. We stepped out and rushed into the middle of the gathering with camera running. I reached my microphone toward Swortha.

"Saun Hoffmann of National Television. Is there any evidence that the prince has been harmed?"

Swortha: "We have no evidence that he has been harmed and are assuming that he is okay."

"Are there any leads on who is responsible?"

Swortha: "Not as of yet; we are following up on everything and we are optimistic that we will soon have something."

"Have you contacted police agencies outside of the country for help?"

Swortha with a sigh: "As of this point, no, but if we see that we can use their help we certainly will."

I asked the obvious question: "Do you know how the kidnappers came in and got out of the grounds?"

Swortha: "That's not information that we can release at this time."

As a journalist, I had to press the issue. "Lord Swortha, the Royal Estate is supposed to be one of the most secure locations in the nation, how is it possible that anyone could have slipped by the system and carried out this crime?"

Swortha, sharply: "I have no comment on that. That's enough, I have to go." With that, he turned to go back into the grounds.

I shouted one more remark after him: "Sir, we know that this must be the hardest day ever in the life of King Alanado and Queen Pristina, would you let them know that the hearts of the whole country are going out to them."

Swortha: "Thank you—I will tell them," he shouted back over his shoulder as he disappeared through the gate.

At that point, Victor Swortha didn't know what his next step was. The gravity of the situation was settling into his emotions. The question about security had especially grated on his nerves. How did someone get past the security? He had little that would give encouragement to the king and the queen. He could only tell them that something would turn up soon; that in 90 percent of all ransom kidnappings, the abductors contact the authorities or the loved ones within the first twelve hours. The media was going to publish the hotline number and ask anyone with information to come forward. It had become a waiting game. They would process the crime scene and contact Interpol for backup support. He reached into his pocket and pulled out a small bottle of aspirin.

I returned to the studio at National Television and reviewed my footage. I had an exclusive that would run prime time around the world, and clips from it could be used over and over for years to come. It was a major break for me, a young reporter trying to advance in the industry. For the previous year, I had been working in the studio and covering an occasional public interest story. That very morning, for lack of something better, I was going to go out with a cameraman to do some footage on migrating geese, if you can believe it. Even though I was low in seniority, I was the only reporter available to take the abduction call when it came in.

I had graduated from college with a degree in journalism and emigrated to Sabothenia from Germany. I was the son of two "literary geniuses," or so they were described by contemporaries. Tragically, I never really knew my parents; they were both killed in a horrible car crash when I was only three. My memories of them were vague at best. I was raised by my father's older brother who had little respect for my dad. Uncle Gradle was an accountant, and had long disrespected his much younger brother's affinity for the literary arts. My mother had met my father at the University of Munich. After their graduation, they had collaborated on two plays that received critical acclaim in West Germany. Their potential was great, but their future was cut short by the tragic accident.

Uncle Gradle was not prone to frivolity, and consequently, I was raised under the strictest of discipline. I was encouraged toward a career in engineering, which Uncle Gradle believed to be appropriate and respectable. But through my younger years, I was drawn to literature and read almost everything I could get my hands on. That was a constant source of contention between me and Uncle Gradle. I was called on the carpet when he discovered a trove of silly stories I had written. I was disciplined harshly and discouraged from engaging in "such foolishness" again.

His constant control and discipline went on throughout my formative years. I became ashamed of my desire to "waste time on such foolishness." One day, Uncle Gradle was approached by one of my teachers who told him I was gifted in literature. The teacher received a severe rebuke and was told, "Saun will be an engineer!" But the occasion had a profound impact on old Uncle Gradle, and after that time I think his heart began to soften. He probably realized he was fighting against my God-given leanings. I was exactly like my dad, and it began to hurt him to think he was hindering his dead brother's only hope of fulfillment. Who was he to stand in the way of a destiny?

As he mellowed he began to drop occasional hints to me that perhaps writing was not such a foolish thing after all. One day he presented me with some of my parents' original writings. That opened a door for me that culminated in my majoring in journalism at the very university my parents had attended.

As a writer, I was drawn to Sabothenia because of the nation's unique history and rich culture. Its history goes back to the time of the Holy Roman Empire. For centuries royal monarchs reigned over Sabothenia's populace. It had been called by historians and political scientists "the land that democracy forgot." The fact that more modern forms of government never gained a foothold in the tiny kingdom had long fueled political debate and speculation the world over. However, it was never a mystery to the country's inhabitants. Their form of government had worked well for so many centuries that they never found cause to change it. They had been ruled by a benevolent dynasty that cared for its people and the people responded in kind.

After arriving there, I spent a couple of years with a newspaper, but was so frustrated with the lack of opportunity for advancement that when an opening came at National Television, I applied for it and got the job. Even though that did not answer my heart's desire, I figured I would have other opportunities to write sometime in the future.

Because of the forthright approach I used with Swortha, the station manager was impressed and assigned me to stake out the Royal Estate. That meant I would be rubbing shoulders with veteran reporters from every other news agency in the world. Over the next year, I would have the opportunity to do exclusives on the investigation and the royal family. I was to become the nation's authority and spokesperson on the subject. When anyone sought the latest on the kidnapping or anything related to it, I became the person to talk to. I truly regretted that such an unfortunate circumstance produced such an invaluable opportunity, but I always felt that it was more than coincidence that it happened to me. That feeling only intensified as I witnessed all of the bizarre details surrounding the case. The saying that "truth is stranger than fiction," certainly applied here, and for a good part of my life, I pondered the subsequent events in amazement. Some say there are forces at work beyond those we can analyze and quantify. They say there is meaning, and purpose in the universe. Because of the things that were revealed as I followed this story, I am inclined to agree.

Chapter 2
SABOTHENIA

Two years after my arrival in Sabothenia, I witnessed a very special event there. From major city to smallest hamlet, every bell that could be rung was ringing. A child, the very first for the popular King Alanado and Queen Pristina, had been born. Every native Sabothenian was tuned in that day; all eagerly crowded around their televisions to catch a first glimpse of the newborn prince. A couple of hours after the birth, his proud father appeared on a balcony of the Royal Mansion with the new prince cradled in his arms. As he raised him up, the crowds standing in the street outside the grounds began to cheer. Prince Renaldo Portance, heir to the throne, was a remarkably beautiful baby. He would never want for any earthly thing. His future seemed as secure as the earth is in its orbit around the sun. Just by being born he would have power, wealth, fame and honor. All was right in the tiny kingdom; or at least it seemed so, on that spring day in 1969.

King Alanado and Queen Pristina, as their ancestors before them, were more than royal figureheads. Their roles involved more than pomp and ceremony; they were actively engaged in the workings of their government. A typical day for them at the Royal Palace involved crisis resolution, international protocol, future planning and public appearances. It was an awesome responsibility and challenge. Government office or "Lordship" as it was called, was granted on the basis of family lines, and to a lesser extent, expertise and qualifications. Nepotism was not a weakness in the nation, however, but a strength. Family honor and name were a check and balance against corruption. Good character was a distinction of the people that served in Sabothenia and that made the whole system work. For over one thousand years it radiated from the top down, making the nation an example of integrity to other evolving societies.

Because honor was taken for granted amongst all the ruling families, breaches were few, but never forgotten. After his coronation, one of King Alanado's first acts was the unpleasant task of removing Lord Durando Poscatal from his position as Administrator of the Budget. A move of that nature was taken only as a last resort, when all remedial efforts had been exhausted. It would also be done in the face of such overwhelming corruption that inaction was not an option. In this particular case, the later condition applied. Evidence was conclusive that Durando had shown favoritism in awarding contracts and had received kickbacks. The king had no choice but to act to maintain public confidence. Durando claimed innocence and said the king had ruined his life. Yet, he immediately went into exile with quite a substantial sum of money. The humiliation and shame brought on the Poscatal family would ease with time, but never be erased. Future generations would not be judged by the faults of their predecessors, but the stain on their reputation would remain as part of the family's ancestral DNA.

It is worth mentioning that poverty was practically nonexistent in Sabothenia. A national economy based on investment banking produced a surplus, year after year. That created a living standard that most nations in the world could only dream of. The country was held in high esteem by the rest of the world, mainly because it was a safeguard of traditional values and old world nostalgia, but its unbridled prosperity was sometimes a challenge for others. It gave some nations, that were founded on more modern forms of government, a bad case of sour grapes. There were only a few countries in the world who had never borrowed money from Sabothenia. Free economies could not understand how a small autocratic nation could be so prosperous, and it was humiliating to be indebted to one. Reality defied reason; a primitive form of government shouldn't have been so successful, but it was.

Tourism ran a strong second to investment banking in making Sabothenia's economy exceptional. Imagine: a thousand-year-old nation, untouched by world wars, filled with thousand-year-old architecture. Sabothenia was not tied up in the Machiavellian web of alliances that had brought about the destruction caused by the First World War. It was saved from the Blitzkrieg of the Second, because Hitler was too cunning to touch a culture so revered by the rest of the world. He knew that if he did, it might cause an outcry that would preempt his designs of world domination. Because its architecture was preserved, it became one of the most coveted places in the world to visit. A classical education was incomplete without a summer in Sabothenia soaking up this antiquated grandeur of ninth century roads, bridges and fortresses. In addition, and even more spectacular, were the hundreds of other preserved structures that were built after that time.

Because of a nostalgic connection to the security of the past, marriages of many famous people took place in the storybook kingdom. Common belief was that the stability of the culture would somehow transfer and become established in a marriage. This idea was fostered and encouraged by many who were positioned to gain financially from its popularization. Trying to capitalize on that perception, Las Vegas, USA, built a theme park based on the layout and cityscape of Sabothenia's capital city, Capriel.

The Royal Palace, the seat of government, was centered in Capriel. It was the main focal point of many ornate government buildings, all of which were surrounded by parks with reflection ponds, fountains, and a variety of manicured trees, flower gardens and lawns. The beauty of the complex has been compared to the Alhambra in Granada. The palace itself was reminiscent of a fairytale castle with spires, turrets, towers and flags. There was a moat around it with a drawbridge at the entrance. The defensive architectural elements had a purpose and had been necessary in the past when the palace was the actual royal residence. Each day at noon a full dress military parade, complete with marching band and cavalry, proceeded into the courtyard of the Royal Palace for the changing of the guard. That event alone was witnessed by an estimated three million tourists every year. Significant affairs of state such as dinners, balls, world summit meetings and coronations took place at the palace.

The beauty and symmetry of Sabothenia's cities did not diminish the splendor of the countryside. The small towns, nestled in rolling hills, had cobbled winding streets lined with thatched-roof stone cottages. Many of the cottages remained as they were hundreds of years before. Tourists wandering through the landscape were enthralled by an emotional experience that could be had few other places in the world.

But the physical characteristics of the country, the history and culture, were all secondary in significance to the people themselves. Most who lived there could trace their ancestry back to the original clans that were believed to have migrated from the Iberian Peninsula as far back as 1500 years before. Legend had it that their forefather, Paternus, was migrating from the south when he was captured by the Visigoths. Paternus showed no fear of his captors and, to the contrary, he tried to befriend them. The Visigoths could not understand that behavior, and their identity as bellicose warriors was threatened by it. Several of their fiercest warriors were captivated by Paternus and were sympathetic towards him. That was seen as a sign of weakness, and their leaders decided that the intruder must be executed as a necessity of survival.

When the judgment was rendered and Paternus was informed of his fate, legend has it that he willingly bowed and bared his neck to his captors. In the place where Paternus fell it was said that a spring of water began to flow. That spring remained in the center of the city of Capriel into modern times. It was the main water supply for the city. Many years ago, the spring was capped and run to reservoirs, and they placed a fountain and a monument over its original location commemorating the legend. It was said that the world-renowned success of orchid growing in Sabothenia was a direct result of that incredible supply of pure spring water, which was claimed to flow directly from the heart of Paternus.

The Sabothenian people, who were rich in national heritage, optimistic, and creative, were second only to African nations as the most repetitious subject of *National Geographic* magazine articles. The richness of their history and culture could always be captured in their faces. Human kindness was a national trait. It was no self-righteous morality, but a genuine heart condition of seeking to do the honest, considerate and decent thing in every situation. Those attributes were not outstanding and praised with each occurrence. They were considered normal behavior. Integrity also prevailed in the justice system. Frivolous lawsuits were practically nonexistent, thereby eliminating the need for excessive liability and other types of insurance that strangled the rest of the world.

So, that was life in Sabothenia, and a very special child prince had just been born there. But the fact is, anyone would be blessed to be born there. If the world was capable of offering a rich and satisfying life, Sabothenia would be the logical place for it to occur. Of course, as we know, the world has no such ability. That would be like saying that canvas and oil paint could create an artist. We know that the issues of life arise from a man's heart; what he sows in life is what makes it great, bearable or intolerable. A dark heart in a perfect world would ruin that world. Unfortunately, we live in a world of many dark hearts. As tranquil and ideal as Sabothenia appeared, darkness lurked there. The world is flawed and darkness is always seeking its way into even the most perfect and envied lives.

Chapter 3
OMENS AND PORTENTS

Of all the history and legends that pervaded Sabothenian culture, there is one theme that persisted. It was the prophesy that one day a star would rise from Sabothenian royal lineage. That person would set a standard of leadership for the entire world. He would be a direct descendent of their forefather Paternus and would dominate the forces of darkness in evil times. The princes born to every generation were thought to be the *rising star*.

It was no exception that the same expectation would be applied to baby Prince Renaldo. But looking at the facts, there was some remarkable alignment between the legend and the circumstances surrounding his birth. Taking a close survey of the evidence gave even conservative thinkers some good conversation around the dinner table. All of that information could be explained as coincidental or normal phenomenon, but it was remarkable enough to stimulate people's imagination and interest.

First, there was the timing of his birth. One ancient prophesy had it that when this leader was born, "a conquered moon would bow her knee to him." People who followed those things found it interesting that later in the same year, the United States conquered the moon when Neil Armstrong stepped on its surface. Many claimed that it was a confirmation. Others claimed that it was a stretch, and if it were the only evidence, then it might have been, but there was more.

March 21, the day of the prince's birth was also the day that all of Sabothenia celebrated the founding of their nation. When their forefather Paternus was killed, his example eventually brought about the conversion of his murderers to Christianity. In the ensuing years, Paternus's clan migrated en mass to the area now known as Sabothenia. His son became the first leader of the people. How the nation's founding came to be celebrated on March 21 was not known, other than the fact that the day also commonly marks the spring equinox. That coincidence was a little more remarkable than the "moon bowing its knee," but it was still not the most convincing argument.

The Church of Sabothenia had very accurate records of past church leaders and their lives. The legend of the *rising star* was considered by the church fathers as more than legend. It was prophesy; and not just one prophesy, but several. There were on record at least eight recorded prophets of the church who had touched upon the subject. They dated back as far as the thirteenth century. They believed that posterity would raise up a leader who would unite a fragmented world in evil times. Many of Sabothenia's church leaders had great faith that the prophesy was being fulfilled. From their ancient documents they knew the man would have great tribulation in his life, but he would overcome it and prevail.

However, the most remarkable item of all of the proposed evidences was his name. Portance was his father's branch of the Paternus dynasty, but Renaldo was his surname given through his mother's side of the family. It was a unique and odd custom for a king and queen to name their firstborn son after the mother's grandfather. That custom generally ensured that kings of Sabothenia would have varied names, rather than repetitious ones. The name Renaldo had long been in Pristina's family, but it was the meaning in the original tribal dialect that enthralled and convinced the church leaders. They were certain the meaning was far beyond coincidence; Renaldo translated as *rising star*! That left no doubt for them. All of this was the preponderance of the evidence; some thought it compelling, some thought it questionable, but all thought it interesting.

Three months of age was the normal time for a baby to be dedicated in Sabothenian religious tradition. The term "christening" was not in their vernacular. They believed in "dedicating" infants as an act of faith, knowing that the child would have to choose for his or herself one day. It was really a time for the parents to make a public vow of their intention to bring their son or daughter up in the teachings of the faith. The tradition applied to average citizens and royalty alike.

When Prince Renaldo reached three months of age, arrangements were made for his dedication. For normal children no special consideration would be required, but for the prince it would be a worldwide media event. It was expected that major TV networks would want camera coverage, so one was selected to provide a feed for all. Other than that, all cameras would be prohibited from the ceremony. There would be a front section in the sanctuary reserved for immediate family members, and dignitaries would be seated behind them. That alone would take one third of the huge cathedral. Many other items and details had been considered for this extraordinary event. The last function of that magnitude had been the marriage of the king and queen fourteen months earlier.

The actual day of the dedication brought a beautiful summer morning in Sabothenia. At the Royal Mansion preparations were being completed. The royal limousine with a police motorcycle escort was awaiting the royal family. And the family was a sight to behold. By then, the prince was at the age where he was perceptive and responding to people. His visible and inner qualities were continuing to develop him into what any observer would recognize as an exceptional child. His parents were the epitome of elegant grace and grandeur; two young rulers who lacked nothing in all the areas people consider of value. They made their way out of the Royal Mansion and into their limo.

They arrived at the church amidst thousands of well wishers.

When the limo came within sight of the immense crowds, the queen exclaimed to her husband, "Oh, look at all these people, and they've all come to honor our prince."

"Yes," the king returned jokingly, "I think he is more popular than we are."

Most of those celebrating the event were outside of the church. Those fortunate enough to be seated inside had been chosen from the regular congregation by lottery to keep it fair. As the royal family proceeded to the front to be seated in their regular place, there was a hush over the entire assembly. Seconds later, the choir rose to fill the building with rapturous praise. During that time, acolytes came forward to light candles, and the minister and his assistants took their positions on the platform. The order of service was praise and worship, normal greeting, baby dedication, a message and, lastly, an invitation.

At the appointed time the king, queen and prince went forward with their family members for the ceremony. The prince was bright and cooing at everyone around him. It was all so perfect. As the king and queen looked out over the gathered admirers, all proceeded smoothly with one small exception. In the center of the congregation a woman was overcome with uncontrollable weeping. Queen Pristina knew the woman. She had high regard for her. She had spoken with her on Sundays and at church functions. She was the wife of one of the deacons. All the church regarded her as a spiritual leader. What on earth had upset her so? Finally, the ceremony and the service concluded. The royal couple left with their dedicated son, to return to their home for a luncheon with family and friends.

In the late afternoon, when the king and queen had retired to private quarters, the queen brought up the subject of the weeping woman.

"Dear, what do you think was wrong with Mrs. Predessa? She was weeping all the way through the dedication."

"It was nothing, sweetheart; she was probably just overcome by the beauty of the ceremony. Some people are just emotional, that's all," the king responded.

"I don't think so; I know her," responded the queen. "I think that there was something more to it than that. I think I'll call her tomorrow and see if she's okay."

The next day, Queen Pristina called the church to get the Predessa's phone number and then dialed it. When Chrissa Predessa answered and found out it was the queen calling, she was immediately upset all over again.

"Chrissa, what is wrong?" the queen asked.

"I am so sorry," Chrissa replied, weeping. "I can't help it."

"You can't help what?" the queen asked.

"The way I feel," Chrissa replied.

"How do you feel?" the queen asked.

"I can't tell you," Chrissa replied.

The queen said, "Chrissa, I want to talk to you. Can I come to see you?"

"Yes, you can come," Chrissa told her. "I am so sorry; I just can't help it."

The queen made arrangements to go to the Predessa home that afternoon and then they hung up. She didn't know what the matter was, but she had to find out. She thought it was an issue that had to do with Chrissa's life in some way, and she wanted to help a friend. Little did she know how much it had to do with her own life.

That afternoon the queen's limo pulled up in front of Chrissa's house. The queen went to the door by herself. Chrissa let her in and led her into a parlor where they could sit. Chrissa's sister had taken the Predessa children for the afternoon.

When they were seated and faced each other, the queen said, "Now tell me what is troubling you."

Again Chrissa apologized in tears and said she just couldn't help the way she felt.

"Explain it to me," the queen said.

"This is very hard and I hope that you will forgive me," Chrissa said, "but it's about the prince."

The queen was surprised by that explanation and she asked "What about the prince?"

"My queen, please forgive me, but I just fear something dreadful is going to happen. I just know that it is, and I have known it ever since the prince was born."

Now Queen Pristina was upset. "What do you mean?" she asked.

"I can't explain it," Chrissa said. "All I know is that since he was born I have had this awful premonition that something terrible is going to happen. I can't escape it; I just know that it's true. Sunday it became more than I could bear, and I just couldn't hold it back."

"What do you think that it is, Chrissa?" the queen asked.

"I don't know, Your Majesty. I've tried to make the feelings go away, but I can't. They just keep getting stronger and stronger." She dissolved into tears again.

The queen was silent for a moment and placed her hand on Chrissa's and told her, "It's going to be all right. I don't know what all of this means, but I know that the prince will be okay. Don't let it bother you any more. I thank you that you have shared it with me. I am sorry that it has been troubling you for so long. But now you need to let it go because you have told me about it."

The queen was speaking out of love and concern for Chrissa, and her words were healing her as they sat there. She didn't know how she would handle the weight that was now on her own heart, but right then she knew that Chrissa needed her encouragement. She told Chrissa that if she learned any more about the feelings she should call the palace and ask to talk to her. Chrissa said she would do that. The meeting had calmed her considerably. She was able to laugh and thank the queen before she left.

But the queen had taken the burden upon herself. All the positive reports and prophesies about the prince that she had heard and fancied were in sharp contrast to the new emotional reality. She felt as if she had been stabbed with a dagger of fear. If it were someone other than Chrissa, she could brush it off, but she knew Chrissa and her family. Chrissa was an honest, sensible person. She was a good mother and wife. Her reputation was excellent in the church. She would never fabricate anything like that. After talking to her, whether it was true or false, she knew that Chrissa believed it to be true with all her heart. Queen Pristina knew from her own experience that there were senses beyond the five that were recognized. It weighed on her emotionally. What did it mean, and what could she do about it?

As soon as the king saw her he asked what the matter was. She told him what had happened.

He said "Come on now; it's going to be okay," the same words that Pristina had used to comfort Chrissa. He said "Whatever it is, and whatever the meaning, we will endure it and overcome it."

As he placed his arms around her, his confidence gradually began to bring some comfort to her. He took the burden from her, and soon she forgot about it, but little did the he know how thoroughly his axiom would be tested.

Chapter 4
THE GRIM REALITY

I tagged along with the station producer one mild Sunday afternoon. The skies were clear and there was a gentle breeze out of the west. We reached our destination to see five black limousines parked in perfect alignment on the tarmac of Capriel International Airport. Uniformed drivers were standing at attention next to their respective vehicles. Within minutes the royal jet touched down and taxied from the runway to the waiting limos; it was a black and gold Boeing 737 with the royal crest on the tail.

When the stairs were in place, the passengers began to disembark. King Alanado and Queen Pristina with relatives, guests, assistants and domestic help, made their way down the stairs, across the pavement and to the waiting open doors of the limousines. A motorcycle escort guided the entourage out of the airport and through the streets to their destinations. Three vans of luggage would follow later. We filmed the episode until the last limo was out of sight. The producer said "Cut, that's a wrap." It would run on the evening news. The people were anxious to know that the king, queen and prince were safely home from their journey.

The Royal Estate was about twelve miles from the airport; far enough to be out of the congestion of the city and somewhat quieter. The grounds encompassed forty acres. The Royal Mansion, a relatively modern building for the country, had been built in the 1850s. It sat in the front and center of the Royal Estate and could be viewed through an eight-foot-high wrought iron fence. There was a gate and security station at that location. The rest of the grounds were contained by a twelve-foot-high stone wall with wrought iron spear points embedded in the top. The twenty-four-room mansion had an exterior of cut granite block with a slate roof. The style of the mansion was the northern European interpretation of Italian Renaissance. Wisteria crept up the exterior walls and bordered several windows.

The estate grounds included the Royal Garden attached to the rear of the mansion and elaborate formal entry gardens between the mansion and the street. The rest of the grounds included lawns with birch, alder, willow and oak trees all planted in a park-like setting. The springtime floral display in the entry garden was a major tourist attraction. Areas not visible to the public were a botanical wonderland. A bridal path, duck pond, tennis courts, indoor swimming pool, and a multitude of other lawn sports facilities completed the appointments. In spite of the relative stability and safety in Sabothenia, concerns in the 1960s mandated a state-of-the-art electronic security system to protect the royal family.

It would be a busy Monday for the king and queen. They had just returned from thirteen days in Japan and the Philippines. The trip involved a state wedding, dedication of a national monument and some other semi-official events. In the Philippines they were received by Ferdinand and Imelda Marcos. This was before Marcos' regime was openly challenged in public and martial law declared. The meeting provided a sharp contrast in monarchies. It became apparent on that visit how little in common the Portance Dynasty had with the Marcos's. The whole trip was salvaged by six days of relaxation and enjoyment in the clear, warm waters around Mindoro Island.

Many people know what it is like to return to work after vacation. Reality descends. Three crises awaited the rulers upon return from paradise. A British diplomat quite close to the

English crown had been treated rudely because of an unfortunate set of circumstances. He had been driving without identification and became involved in an accident with a public transportation vehicle. The diplomat had alcohol on his breath and the officer at the scene cuffed him and took him to jail. It was later determined, quite to the embarrassment of the police department, that, as he had told them, he did have diplomatic immunity and his blood-alcohol level was quite below the legal limit.

The second crisis involved the air pollution from surrounding industrial nations. It had caused severe conditions because of an air inversion. Over one hundred elderly persons and numerous children had been admitted to hospitals for treatment. One elderly woman had died. Normally, Sabothenia was protected from that condition by the prevailing wind pattern and it was never known to have happened before. The negative press that resulted caused a severe dip in tourism. Numerous cancellations meant a loss of income for hundreds of families whose livelihoods were dependent on foreign visitors.

The third catastrophe was a train wreck that highlighted the nation's archaic rail system. A complete revamping of the national railroad had been planned and budgeted and was to be implemented over a period of twelve years, but the crash made it apparent that a much faster, more radical, overhaul would have to be performed.

Those are the types of issues that face nations and cities every day all over the world, but when dumped in your lap on the first day back, it can be somewhat daunting. Fortunately, solutions had been worked out before the king and queen's return so it was mostly a matter of briefing and then selection of final plans of action. That is life in leadership. The reassuring aspect of these crises was the fact that each had a solution. Perhaps there was cause to make one wonder if there was really any problem that could not be fixed with the proper amount of attention and money. Unfortunately, life had dealt Alanado and Pristina a great disservice by lulling them into believing that they were immune to consequences or tragedy. Who would have believed that three days later the queen would be coiled in a chair, sobbing convulsively and experiencing what any psychologist would call a normal reaction to the her circumstance.

The queen rose up and lashed out in frustrated anger.

"I can't believe that this has happened," she yelled at her husband. Then, collapsing back into tears, "I want my baby!" Then, in anger again, "How could the security staff have been so inept? What are the police doing to get my baby back?"

With each turn of emotion, Alanado hovered over her, trying to calm her. Then she fell on the bed in tears again. At that point the queen's mother and father arrived and stood outside the Royal Chambers asking to come in. Alanado opened the door to them and they rushed in to embrace Pristina. Alanado left the queen in their hands and went out to meet with Victor Swortha.

Swortha went through his well rehearsed talking points of encouragement. "We should hear something within the next few hours. They are probably waiting for the optimum time to make contact and when they do, we will have them. We will trace the call and do our best to take them into custody."

The king responded hotly, "You will do nothing without my approval. Whatever they want I am willing to give them.

Whatever! Do I make myself clear? You will do nothing to jeopardize the well-being of my son."

"Absolutely, Your Majesty," Swortha replied. "You will have final say on everything that we do and we will do nothing without your approval."

Victor Swortha's son Eduardo, was one of the detectives working at the scene. He was also one of the king's athletic competitors in college. Because of that, Victor knew the young king fairly well. He was sensitive to his state of mind and bore no resentment for his agitation and shortness with him. He only wished he had more information to give him. He was hoping for a break in what would probably be the most urgent and compelling case of his life. He thought of all his training and discipline in law enforcement and realized how inadequate it was. He was at the mercy of sinister forces that had complete control of the situation.

He tried to calm himself and keep a cool head for when the next phase of this crime would unfold. He returned to his car and began to jot down notes. A command center had been set up in the library of the Royal Mansion. After fifteen minutes alone and three more aspirin, he went back in to confer with his men.

All was in place. The Central Bank had been put on alert for a large sum of cash, possibly in the one million dollar range. Tellers were counting and bundling the cash for delivery. Surveillance and backup were at the ready for deployment to any site within the country. Medical teams were on alert for immediate dispatch. Every possibility he could think of was covered. His detectives who processed the crime scene came to inform him they had found nothing of value. The staff interviews also produced nothing of value. Officers who combed the immediate neighborhoods and interviewed residents uncovered nothing of value. Everything hung in the balance on the anticipated contact. Swortha was holding none of the cards in his hand, and he had never felt more vulnerable in his life.

The hours continued to mount…four hours, eight hours, twelve hours. No phone call, no note, no contact. The story had hit the wires and it was the lead story of evening news broadcasts worldwide. Every peace-loving person in the free world was aghast and hoped for a good outcome. The phone and wire communications from world leaders had begun to pour in. Psychics with conflicting premonitions were numerous. Swortha enlisted the national telephone company operators to field the many public phone calls to the police. Tips were coded by color: red was "urgent," green was "possible importance," yellow was "irrelevant," and blue was "well-wisher." By the twenty-fourth hour after the kidnapping there were eighteen code red calls that had been checked out and found to be without merit. Every person in Sabothenia wanted to help in some way to fix this horrible tragedy. The most astounding thing was the fact that they'd had no contact from the abductors.

Swortha was bearing the brunt of the pressure from every direction. The king and queen were looking to him for an answer and the public was relentless. It seemed the good character of the nation was being tested and the predictable second guessing and accusations had already started flying. Wasn't the National Police Force in charge of the security at the Royal Estate? How could they have been so inept?

Examination of how the crime was committed was still in process, but a general theory was beginning to emerge. There was a previously unknown flaw in the security. There was one small location in the formal garden that was without camera coverage. How could anyone have known about the flaw? How did they evade the electronic sensors to get into the grounds and get out without being detected? Someone got in and was waiting for the governess and the prince. When and how they did it, no one knew. How they scaled the wall to get in and out, no one knew. There was no one person to blame; it was just an oversight that someone with great sophistication exploited. Perhaps the greatest weakness in the security was the fact that no one ever expected anything like that could or would occur in Sabothenia.

Help was offered from the major law enforcement and intelligence agencies in the Western world. Top secret information of the most sensitive nature was reluctantly divulged by the CIA in the United States. The information, if revealed, could have jeopardized free world domination in the Cold War, because it involved technology that was not even known to exist at that time. It was made available to Swortha by a direct order of the President of the United States, Richard M. Nixon. Swortha because of his law enforcement reputation and personal friendship with the president was counted as trustworthy.

Interestingly enough, the CIA had a satellite passing over Capriel at the time of the kidnapping. One image showed a solitary figure approaching the wall from the inside of the Royal Estate. The image was captured at exactly 10:11 a.m. on the day of the kidnapping. Though it was not intelligence that Swortha could share, it was helpful to him to know the kidnapping was carried out by a solitary individual. Who was the man, where did he go, and what was his plan? Why had he made no attempt to contact the king or the authorities for ransom? Those were questions that remained unanswered. Forty-eight hours had passed without any contact from him.

The king and the queen made a public appeal to the kidnappers from the library of the Royal Mansion. I was there to direct the crew that went in to do the taping. Many claimed it was truly the saddest television interview that had ever been broadcast. What was considered by all to be an enviable life of dignity, poise and majesty had become a life of tragedy and desperation for the king and queen. Beautiful Queen Pristina, with a face revealing the torment of her situation, pled for mercy from the people who had her son. She revealed she would give anything, even her own life for the return of her child. She said, "Whatever you require, we will do, just please don't harm my son," and then dropped her head into her hands and sobbed convulsively.

The king followed by giving his word that arrangements would be made to maintain the abductor's anonymity. "We just want our son back. No questions will be asked and no attempt will be made to capture."

After the filming, as the queen was leaving the room, she stopped and thanked me for what she believed to be a sensitive approach to the interview. I thanked her and told her I wished I could do more to help.

As a sad commentary on humankind, several ransom requests were made and deemed to be false. The frauds were unable to answer specific details about the crime. Criminal prosecution was turned over to the nations where the false attempts originated. The true kidnapper remained silent. Three days had passed.

The king and queen were drawn to each other as the nightmare unfolded. Never in their most horrific imaginings could they have anticipated or prepared for the fear that tried to overpower them. They had lived the perfect life up to that point, ordered lives that were proper and dignified, lives where nothing unseemly, violent or frightening ever took place. They had grown up in the church where all things were explained and accounted for. They knew all the proper religious terminology, but those phrases were of little comfort to them in the present circumstance. They were treading virgin soil.

Their pastor came to pray with them, but he was little help. He was convinced it was his responsibility to prepare them for the inevitable bad news that they would eventually have to face. That's what he tried to do, but he found no receptivity and went away frustrated. The help they were seeking seemed to be beyond the reach of their traditional religious setting. None of their friends or relatives really knew how to talk to them either. The young ruling monarchs who were formerly the toast of the world, had never felt so alone and isolated. So they drew close and encouraged each other to try and keep their focus positive.

Chapter 5
ALL THE KING'S HORSES

Two weeks had passed with no break in the case, but the king and queen resisted the thoughts and looks on the faces of those around them. They desperately sought a means of maintaining strength in the face of the overwhelming odds against them. They started to see flaws in the charmed life that had left them so ill-prepared for their circumstance. Contrary to what they had always believed, they had come to see there are things beauty, royalty and money cannot fix. There had to be something more than what they had always relied on. There are realities in life that demand something greater than the best solutions that the world has to offer. The brightest minds of Scotland Yard, the FBI and the CIA could not come up with a motive for the crime. The most advanced intelligence and law enforcement techniques could not develop a lead. Tracking dogs could not pick up a scent. The crime scene had been processed and reprocessed by the best, without results. If they were ever to see their son again, it was going to take something greater than what men's efforts had to offer.

Swortha withheld most of the discouraging facts from the parents. He knew they did not want to hear it, but he couldn't deny the odds were against recovering the prince alive. His professional guess was they would never see their son again. It was probably a botched crime. He surmised the prince had not survived the abduction, and the abductor had disposed of the child's body and was in hiding. The weeks went on: three weeks, one month.

The baby's room was left untouched. Each night, one of the security staff made his midnight rounds in the Royal Mansion.

It became a common experience for him to see a light coming from under the door to the prince's room. The first time he saw the light he immediately opened the door to find the king and queen on their knees praying. He apologized and excused himself. For the next few nights, he quietly opened the door to check, but from then on, he checked every room except for that one. He knew who was there and he didn't disturb them. The royal couple were taking their pursuit for answers to a higher level.

At the end of that first month, the king had returned to his duties as ruler of the realm; he didn't want to do it, but it was imperative. The wellbeing of the nation was dependent upon his position on the throne. It was a year before the queen appeared in public. It was during that first year that the heart of the people of Sabothenia could really be seen. No one could remember a time in the past that had tested them so severely. Though most people thought the worst had probably happened, the support the Royal family received from them was remarkable. Women in the realm would have given their own children to replace the one lost.

At the end of one year the queen offered a televised interview to Barbara Masters of American television. The viewing ratings for the program were second only to Neil Armstrong's walk on the moon the summer before. The queen made one small request, that I be allowed to do the interview with Barbara. The reason she gave was that my handling of the story over the previous year had been "sensitive and considerate of the royal family."

The night of the taping, the queen was radiant. All who admired her were amazed to see she had retained her former persona of beauty and dignity, tempered with engaging personal warmth. Where did she get such charm and grace? She was the epitome of what the entire world knew to be

Sabothenian. But there was a new something about her, I could see it. It was a new kind of assurance or confidence that I had begun to notice over the previous year. During the interview, the source of that strength became known to the world.

Barbara Masters: "Ladies and gentlemen, I'm Barbara Masters of NBC along with Saun Hoffmann of Sabothenia National Television. We're here tonight to spend some time with Her Majesty, Queen Pristina Portance." The camera panned to include all three of us as Barbara continued to talk. "Your Majesty, thank you so much for agreeing to chat with us; you know that the hearts and minds of the world have been with you this past year. There are millions watching this interview that have been longing to know how you are, and just seeing you will set them at ease."

Queen Pristina: "Thank you, Barbara. I thought it was time to let the world know that I am all right. We have been blessed and encouraged by thousands upon thousands of people who have sent cards and letters to express their concern and sympathy over the situation."

Barbara Masters: "Queen Pristina, can I start by sharing a question given to me by a young girl in the United States? Lisa Robinson wants to know if it was a difficult decision for you to give up a career in the theater to become queen."

Queen Pristina: "Well actually, no it wasn't, Lisa. I knew I could become an actress, but I didn't know I could become a queen. I had a childhood dream that Prince Alanado would ask me to marry him, as we knew each other from the time we were very young. When he asked me, it was very easy because I realized it was what I really wanted all my life. I have never had any regrets about that decision."

Then the floor director cued me for my question. "Your Majesty, I want to thank you for making yourself available to the many people who care so much about you. I want to let you know that over the past year I have been asked thousands of questions, but the majority of the questions are about you and your wellbeing."

Queen Pristina: "It is a tremendous responsibility to carry, that so many are involved and interested in my life, Saun. I just hope I can continue to live up to their expectations and not let them down. And I want to thank you for the excellent job you have done reporting the events of the past year. The king and I both watch you daily, and are grateful for your sensitive and considerate approach."

For Barbara, the interview was off to a great start. When she was given the assignment there was trepidation because of the difficulty in dealing with such a sensitive issue on camera. However, the queen's professional demeanor was making it very easy to get some wonderful footage. But now the challenge was to steer the subject in the direction of what the world would tune in to hear about. After some more casual conversation, Barbara decided to take the plunge with the sensitive but forthright approach she was famous for.

Barbara Masters: "Queen Pristina, I think everyone wants to know what it has been like for you over the past year. Can you shed some light on that?"

Queen Pristina: "The first couple of weeks were the worst. The tension was more than we could bear, the not knowing and the waiting. Finally, when it began to look like we were not going to get an immediate answer, we had to start dealing with the kidnapping on a more long-term basis. I knew that the best thing for my child was to keep my wits and my faith that he is okay, and that he will be reunited with us. And that is what I decided to do."

I knew the king and queen had never given up hope that the prince was still alive, but the answer somewhat stunned Barbara, and she was noticeably taken by surprise. She, along with everyone else, had assumed the king and queen believed the prince must be dead by this time. She was astonished that the queen believed the prince was still alive and that she would see him again. Barbara struggled to come up with the proper response, and while not the best of her career, it was all she could think of.

Barbara Masters: "Your Majesty, do you *really* believe someone is holding the prince and will still release him to you?"

Queen Pristina, with a slight tremor in her voice: "I absolutely do. There is something in me that refuses to believe Renaldo is not alive. There is no evidence one way or the other, and I choose to believe he is. If there is such a thing as women's intuition, and I believe there is, that sense in me says I will see him again in this life. For most of the past year, that has been my hope and because of that hope I am not in despair. If a day should come that I find out differently, then I shall mourn, but until that day, I will believe for him and pray for him daily. And I must ask that if anyone is watching this program and knows of anything that will help the investigation, I beg you to contact our National Police."

I added to her comment: "Yes, Your Majesty, and I want to add that a one-hundred-thousand-dollar reward for any information leading to the recovery of the prince, still stands. Also, I want to assure you that the rest of this nation is believing for a good outcome right along with you."

Now Barbara was reeling, she could not believe what she had heard. She was struggling to keep her composure and respond without surprise or unbelief in her tone. She thought she had come to console the queen and that is what she had rehearsed. She was off balance and all she could come up with to recover was to praise the queen for her great faith.

Barbara Masters: "Your Majesty, I must admit I am amazed at your great strength and faith, and I am sure it is an example to everyone who has faced similar tragedy."

Queen Pristina, with tears in he eyes: "Barbara, you need to know that someone greater than myself and my husband is watching over our son, and that is where our trust is. We will continue in that trust, and I have an inner peace and assurance that we will not be disappointed."

On that note, the director gave Barbara the "cut" signal. Not only was he objecting to the direction of the discussion, but their time was up. We said our polite thank-yous and goodbyes. When the interview ran on TV, many people just sat in front of their sets pondering what the queen had said. Some thought, what an amazing woman with an amazing will. Others were offended by what they called "religious crap." Psychologists believed her to be mentally disturbed because of the abduction. Most prime-time television personalities did not comment on the queen's statement, but columnists and late night talk shows were not as polite. The word "denial" probably came into everyday vernacular because of their analysis. They were entitled to their opinion, but in 1971 most people wanted to believe along with the queen. Certainly the people of Sabothenia would try, at least for awhile.

There was someone else that watched the interview that night who was also noted for having a strong will. It was Victor Swortha. He sat in his office at the National Police Force headquarters, taking notes and recording his thoughts. His will was not set on finding the prince alive, however. It was set on bringing to justice the one who was responsible for the felony. If believing for the prince's return was a passion for the king and queen, then catching the criminal was a passion for Swortha. He was not obsessed at that point, but he was getting close. He was overly determined. He lived and breathed in the hope that there would be a break in the case that would lead to an arrest. It was all very personal for him. The unsolved crime was the only blemish on his long and distinguished career. One day, somehow, he would get a break in the case. It was just a matter of time for him, and he was willing to pursue it until it happened.

Chapter 6
ROOTS OF THE TREE

While the NBC interview tarnished the queen's image with some, it pushed her over the top for others. The approval came from quarters that were not so caught up in the content as they were in the celebrity. The derogatory description could be "royalty groupies" and the complimentary one would be "fans." But there is no denying that Queen Pristina had a following. She was beautiful, intelligent, engaging and glamorous and undoubtedly, one of the most popular women in the world. She came by a certain amount of that naturally, but there was also a portion that came through proximity and training. The proximity part was the fact that she knew the king since their childhood; the training part from the advantage of having grown up leading a charmed life.

She was born Pristina Deanna Ocassa. Her father, Provinso Ocassa, was credited with bringing Sabothenia into the prominence it enjoyed as a world travel destination. He was indeed, a hard worker who came by his fortune honestly. As a young man, Provinso was positioned to observe the effectiveness of propaganda used by all sides during WW2. He was fascinated by the fact that one poster with an effective slogan could accomplish more than hours of rhetoric. He recognized the positive potential of that medium, and he envisioned its use in another application; it could be used to promote commerce.

Sabothenia's postwar economy was sagging along with the rest of Western Europe. Provinso was inspired to start his own propaganda campaign by placing small weekly ads in the *New York Times*. It was a simple ad depicting the Royal Palace in

Capriel with the caption "Romance Survives in Sabothenia." Beneath that, he had the contact information for the tour company he founded. Before long, he was contacted by a travel agency in the United States. It was slow to pick up, but within two years, he was booked fulltime and expanding. Eventually, his agency became the clearinghouse for all tourist activity in Sabothenia. Every hotel, limousine service, restaurant and entertainment facility was paying Provinso. By the age of thirty, he was one of the wealthiest men in the nation.

Pristina's mother, Amelia, was beautiful and talented and sang in the opera. Provinso courted and married her and their first child, Pristina, was born in 1948. She was raised in an atmosphere of celebrity and privilege. She was beautiful from birth and as she grew, her large expressive eyes were baby blue and her hair grew long and blond. There was more to Pristina than her natural looks; however, she was a most peaceful child. He parents could not remember ever disciplining her; perhaps she received a spanking once or twice in her entire childhood. She emanated peacefulness to the extent that people remarked about it. Her clear blue eyes were piercing and daunting to some, but when visitors got beyond the initial impact, they discovered a personality that was warm and engaging.

At four years of age, her parents placed her in a private school which the royalty of the nation attended. It just so happened that young Alanado Portance, the Crown Prince and son of King Marsalis and Queen Chrystallina, was also enrolled there. The two children were classmates and became friends. This brought their parents into a relationship, which was unusual considering the contrast between new money and aristocracy. King Marsalis was not one to stand on protocol and the queen had long admired Amelia. It was at the prince's fifth birthday celebration that both sets of parents noticed Alanado's connection with Pristina was stronger than it was with his other playmates who attended. It was important to Alanado that Pristina be seated next to him and he insisted she receive the first piece of birthday cake.

Their friendship continued beyond the school year and they rode horses and swam together in summertime. It was not uncommon for one or the other to spend part of a weekend with the other's family. It was a natural mutual attraction. They were like brother and sister. It wasn't that she was a tomboy or that he was effeminate, they were just drawn to the common ground of mutual interests. Pristina's parents were often invited to royal functions, which would never have happened had it not been for the children's relationship.

When they got to be around eleven years of age, it all ended. At first, parents on both sides were mystified. Provinso and Amelia reasoned that it was childhood wisdom in action; the children somehow knew that they were approaching puberty and their friendship could no longer continue as it had been. It was like some unspoken rule or barrier that demanded their relationship change. When asked about the cooling, neither had much to say about it. Pristina told her parents, "Oh, I don't know, we never really liked each other that much anyway." Alanado told his parents that he was just friends with Pristina because they had befriended her parents.

Both of the children developed other friendships and other interests. The new friendships were same sex, which seemed to be more acceptable to both sets of parents anyway, so the subject was dropped. Amelia had always been interested in nurturing Pristina's talent and hoped she would sing. The change in relationship provided more time to focus on that goal. Coaching did not produce the spectacular results that her mother had hoped for, however. Pristina had the looks and grace for the opera, but not the singing voice.

Pristina was interested in movies. She told her mother that she wanted to be a movie star. In that day, movie stars were not so celebrated in Sabothenia, which was more conservative and inclined to the classical theater. Her mother told her she could act, but not in film. She said that movie acting would not be appropriate for a young woman of her standing in Sabothenia. He mother pushed her in the direction of becoming a stage actress. Pristina eventually consented and her training began.

At the same time Alanado, like most of the boys his age, was aspiring to be an athlete. He had the strength and physique for it. Even at the age of eleven and twelve, his shoulders were broad and his chest tapered to his waist. His dark brown hair and the determined set of his green eyes spoke of vitality and life. He played soccer, he wrestled and he ran track and field. Never did he use his social position to give him undeserved advantage. He was a true competitor and did his father proud. He needed no assistance or preferential treatment and he sweated and bled with all the other boys who aspired to be the best. From that time on, Alanado chose his friends from the ranks of his competitors. He mostly looked up to those who were his greatest challenge on the field. Other than his education, competitive sports occupied most of his waking moments.

As Alanado excelled in that pursuit and established himself as a prodigious athlete, Pristina pursued her interests on the stage. She took ballet and mime in Paris as disciplines to round out her skill. At fourteen years of age, she acted her first role in a production called *Some Will Call*. It was the story of a family of disadvantaged girls growing up in 1930s Spain. Pristina played the fourth oldest sister in a family of seven. It was far from the lead role, but she did receive some exposure and it opened doors for her. By the time she was sixteen, she was routinely doing supporting roles and had a name for herself as a child actress. One year later, she played a lead opposite the German stage actor, Froust Gogel. That role brought her acclaim beyond Sabothenia. The play toured Europe to sold-out audiences. She was considered exceptional for a seventeen year old.

Contact between Alanado and Pristina after their preadolescent split was limited to occasional sightings. One time they passed each other at an event and smiled and nervously said hello. It was awkward for them. They both felt like there should have been more, considering how close they had been in the past, so it was embarrassing. They knew each other's childhood secrets, which was forbidden knowledge in a teenager's world. Some things were better pushed to the back of the mind, and the last thing either of them wanted was to be around someone who remembered them. The situation happened again a couple of months after that, but that time Pristina was prepared and casually asked Alanado how he was doing. He told her that he was doing well and he asked the same of her. They parted and that was the last time they spoke for a few years.

It wasn't until Alanado was seventeen that he asked his parents why they no longer invited the Ocassas to any functions.

His father smiled knowingly to his mother and said, "Well, son, I don't really know, but it has been on my mind to reestablish that relationship. Thank you for reminding me."

The next formal event was a state ball held in honor of a visiting dignitary and his wife. The Ocassas were invited and Alanado was there, dressed and ready to see Pristina, but she didn't come with them. When he found that out, he left early, returned to his room and went to bed.

On the next occasion, which also happened to be a ball, Alanado was prepared once more. That time Pristina came with her parents. He was struck dumb by her incredible beauty.

He had seen recent photos of her because of her stage career, but seeing her in person ran his emotions through their paces. A good hour into the evening, when he had finally worked up the nerve to approach her, she was gracious and receptive to his advance. They danced together. At the end of the evening, feeling much more confident because of her friendliness, he asked if she would consider seeing him sometime in the future. She told him she would be very pleased to see him.

Alanado, along with his parents, were invited to see her perform in her most current role. After the play, he waited backstage with flowers.

When she came out from the dressing area, there were two other male actors with her. As soon as she saw Alanado, she stopped in her tracks as if she were alone. The young men with her continued walking and talking, then realizing that she was no longer with them, turned and looked back to see her standing as if in a trance. Her eyes were fixed on Alanado, and suddenly it seemed to her as if they had never been apart. It was a deja vu experience for her. She saw the same personality that had drawn her at preschool many years before. They both stood wondering why they had ever stopped being friends. It was there in the backstage area that she believed she would become his wife and it would be such a natural transition. It was clear that it had always been meant to be. But she could never have known, at that moment, the long trial that marriage to the prince would produce.

Chapter 7
HOPE DEFERRED

About four years after the kidnapping, Victor Swortha retired from his post as Lord of the National Police Force. He was replaced by his son Eduardo Swortha. His retirement did not apply to the kidnapping of the prince, however. He would never give up his determination to bring the perpetrator to justice. He used his influence to secretly keep the investigation alive, even though for all intents and purposes the case was closed. If the truth be known, his real reason for retirement was to have more time to spend on the investigation, and now it could receive his full attention. He was consumed by it.

He began by pouring over government documents and files. One area of research had to do with security at the Royal Mansion. He found reference to a security evaluation of the Royal Estate that was performed in 1966. No copies of that evaluation could be found on record anywhere. Through an interview with a retired security employee he found the evaluation had been performed by an auditor named Longo Natras who ran a small security consulting business in Capriel. Not only was the evaluation missing, but so was Longo Natras. He could find no record of the company or the man later than 1967. Eventually, he received a tip that Natras was living in Belgium under another name.

Swortha traveled to Brussels and began his search. Because of his connections, he had local law enforcement help. Natras was located and brought in by the police for an interview on an unrelated charge for. When Natras saw Swortha it was obvious he was agitated. He was reticent to talk to Swortha, but when he found out how much Swortha knew he began to open up.

"I did the security audit. What about it?"

"I see in your report that it revealed a blind spot in the camera coverage of the garden," Swortha said. This was a bold step considering that Swortha had never seen the report.

"Yeah, there was a flaw," Natras confirmed.

"Who did you do the report for?" Swortha asked.

"I don't think that I want to say any more about this, and I don't think that you have anything to hold me on."

That was the last thing Natras said, and he would say no more. It was obvious he was afraid of someone. The Brussels police had to release him. The next day Natras disappeared. The police entered his apartment to find it was in shambles; someone had to have been looking for something. What it was, and whether they found it or not, was a mystery.

Swortha knew he had finally gotten the break he had been seeking, but his only source of information had vanished. He was allowed to examine the apartment. After several hours of sifting through the debris he found an old calendar with the initials "DP" written in on the date of the prince's kidnapping. A month later a body surfaced in the canal with a bullet hole in the head. The police believed it to be Natras, but decomposition was too severe to obtain a positive identification.

Swortha thought about what he had: 1. A hushed-up security report with no copies anywhere in government records, 2. The report itself possibly revealed the very flaw in security that had been exploited to kidnap the prince, 3. The person who completed the report disappeared under suspicious circumstances and had probably been murdered, and 4. A calendar found in the disappeared man's apartment with the initials "DP" written in on the date of the prince's abduction.

It wasn't too difficult for him to come up with a plausible scenario. He believed the "DP" stood for Durando Poscatal, the former Lord of the Budget who was removed from office by King Alanado. He had considered Poscatal before but had absolutely nothing to substantiate his suspicion. Poscatal certainly had the power to order a security evaluation and to keep it secret. But why would he have a security report completed two years before he was actually removed from office? Was he anticipating his removal from office and preparing for revenge or just keeping something he could use in some way for some reason? At any rate, after his removal from office, Poscatal probably planned the kidnapping and carried it out. The theory gave the first plausible motive for a crime that had been without explanation for over four years.

Victor Swortha said goodbye to his wife at the airport and boarded a flight to go back to Brussels to try and find Poscatal. He had been informed by the Poscatal family that Durando was probably there. Swortha landed in Brussels and checked into a hotel. That was the last time anyone ever saw him. Unfortunately, he left no notes on what he had found. His choices were very unprofessional. He had written a couple of papers advising against such behavior, but he became so caught up with his investigation, that he got careless.

The day that Victor Swortha left, some employees at the Royal Mansion were sitting around the servants' table in the kitchen having midmorning tea. Dora, one of the housekeepers, was remarking about Her Highness, the Queen. She said she had seen the queen in the Royal Garden talking to herself at the grave. She was immediately corrected by Sophia, the head of housekeeping, who overheard her comment. "I have told you not to call the shrine in the garden a grave, and why would you assume that Her Majesty was talking to herself?"

"I'm sorry, ma'am" Dora replied. "I forgot about what you said, and it just looked like Her Majesty was talking to herself."

Sophia continued, "When Her Majesty goes to the garden, she could be praying, she is not talking to herself. And if she should speak to her lost son, what is that to you?"

"I didn't mean anything by it," Dora replied. "I beg your pardon, ma'am. It's just that some people say it's time for Her Majesty to let go of the prince and not assume he will be coming back."

Sophia corrected her again, but very sharply. "What some people say is of no concern to you, Dora! You are a servant in the royal household, and it is your job to clean and keep your comments to yourself!"

Dora lowered her eyes and said, "Yes, ma'am."

It's true that the king and the queen's position on their son was not understood by many. At first it was, but after such a long time most people began to give up hope. But whose business was it, if the king and queen wanted to believe their son might still be alive? Queen Pristina was the mainstay of the belief. She said she knew it in her heart. King Alanado was encouraged by her. He had known her most of his life, and when she believed something, he had learned it usually turned out to be correct. But it was a stretch. It was against all odds. How could it be true? All of the facts, all of the experts, and all of common sense was against them. Most people after that much time just shook their heads when they thought about the king and queen's "fantasy."

The royal couple's passion in the area did not wane with time, but grew stronger. They longed to know the truth and see their son again. They were desperate for it and the nightly sessions in the prince's room continued. Some said they just could not face the alternative. The truth was too painful, and it would destroy them. Many believed that one day they would have to face up to it. Queen Pristina was willing to face the truth, but something inside had convinced her that the prince was alive. She and King Renaldo continued to encourage each other, and their alliance drew them closer than would have ever been possible had they never experienced the tragedy.

Their lives did go on. They had two more children. It seemed as though time in Sabothenia came to be measured in terms of the disappearance of the prince. Lorraine was born a year and a half after the disappearance. Julia was born four years later. There was a storm of gossip over a comment made by Queen Pristina after the birth of Julia. When an insensitive visitor who had a little too much wine commented in her presence about there being no male heir to the throne, the queen replied, "How do you know that there is no male heir?" Then she abruptly left the room with her guests standing there. Her comment created a stir, but people soon forgot about it.

The king and queen also had to cope with tabloid headlines like: "LOST PRINCE FOUND" or "PRINCE RENALDO SEEN AT ROYAL ESTATE." But that is normal for famous personalities. Actually, their lives were really very normal, or at least as normal as the life of a royal family can be. Their children were at the center of their life. Lorraine was blond and blue-eyed like her mother. Julia was a brunette with green eyes like her father. While Lorraine was organized and deliberate and predictable, Julia was precocious and a handful. Their parents were blessed by their children and the world was speculating if there would be more, but it didn't happen.

Eventually people assumed that Lorraine would be the next queen. The years passed.

Chapter 8
THE SUBSTANCE OF THINGS HOPED FOR

As previously mentioned the royal couple were very active in the affairs of state, but they were also quite active socially. After the kidnapping, however, their activism moved in a new direction. You might say they became involved in benevolent causes. They had always written generous checks for charity, but in the years following the kidnapping, they became personally involved.

The queen spent time working in children's services. As the twentieth century ground on, world trends began to have an impact on Sabothenia. A nation that once had at no stats on divorce was in the throes of an epidemic of failed marriages. Drugs and alcohol were also an issue in the nation and contributed to the condition. The queen became an advocate for the children affected by divorce and oversaw a national advocacy program. It was a natural for her to be concerned with children because of her experience with the plight of her own son, but there was something else about it that drew her and revived her; it was the tenderness and hope that she saw in the depth of a child's heart. A child will believe beyond what circumstances would indicate is possible. This was something she could relate to. The faith and trust of small children insulated them, to a certain extent, from the brutal realities of life.

To many, Queen Pristina came to exemplify the virtues of faith and trust in the face of overwhelming adversity. Around the world, women came to look to her example in that area. Many of them were seeking loved ones, mainly children, who had disappeared without a trace. She was an encouragement to them. She wrote poetry for her own enjoyment, but in the 1980s she released a collection for publication. She wanted to get it in the hands of those that it could encourage. Though it was intended for women who shared her plight and sought comfort, it immediately became a best seller. There were forty-six poems, ranging from three pages long to a few lines. All of them had a theme of optimism and hope, and some revealed a spiritual depth well beyond what anyone would expect from an actress turned queen.

Those activities were considered appropriate for the queen and she was admired for them. King Alanado also had some humanitarian projects for which he was admired. Once people got used to the idea, his example set a standard for the entire nation. Why shouldn't royalty humble themselves and give of their time for social causes? All of it was fine until four years after the kidnapping when he made a trip to the National Prison. He only went there to encourage the inmates, but it was viewed by many as extremely inappropriate for the king of the nation. Shortly after his visit, Lord Wensel Prosonni, administrator of the Sabothenian Social Services was pushed forward by several others to speak to the king about it.

After a routine staff meeting he asked Alanado if he could have a private word with him. The two of them retreated to the king's office and closed the door behind them.

Lord Prosonni cleared his throat and nervously said, "Your Majesty, there have been a lot of comments made about your activity last week."

"What activity are you talking about, Wensel?"

"Sir, the one at the prison. Many people are very upset that you went there. They think that you have brought disgrace on the monarchy."

"Well, they do, do they? What you think, Wensel?"

"Sir, Of course you know that I greatly admire all of the things that you and Queen Pristina have done to help the less fortunate, but I'm not so sure about that one. Why would you go there to be around those people? They're criminals, sir. Some of them hate the monarchy. They've all been convicted of crimes; some are of the most horrible nature. Why would you spend your time with people like that?"

The king sighed and shook his head. "Wensel, don't I see you and your family in church every week? Why do you go there?"

"Well, sir, I go there to be encouraged."

"Have you ever thought that 'those people' need to be encouraged as well?"

"Sir, we have counselors there to do that. We have a very humane system. They are well provided for, sir. I make sure of that."

"Alright, that's true, but let me put it to you this way then; do you think that Jesus would go there?"

"Of course he would have, sir, but he wasn't the king of the...nation..."

As Lord Prosonni said "king of the nation," he dropped his eyes, and his words trailed off into awkward silence. His face flushed, and he looked up at the king with a sheepish smile. That was the last the king ever heard about his trips to the prison. He did it a couple of times each year after that, and no one ever mentioned it again, at least to his face.

In the late twentieth century Sabothenia's prison was more of a need than when it was originally built. After the '60s the nation had changed significantly for the worse. "The perfect country" had developed a significant crime problem. The royal visits had been a very productive effort; many men there respected him and appreciated the fact that he cared enough to come and see them. They listened to him as he shared a message. Usually it had to do with believing for things that average people thought to be impossible.

On one particular occasion, eighteen years after the abduction, the king was greeted by the lieutenant who informed him of the man they had on death row. The king said he had been following the story in the papers.

"This is the man who killed a policeman, isn't it?" the king asked.

"That is correct," the lieutenant replied. "His name is De Honden. I don't know what that means, but he is the worst we have ever had here. There are some other inmates that would like to get their hands on him. Some of us here think we should let them have him and save the cost of the execution."

The king ignored his ill humor and asked if he could see the young man. The lieutenant took him by the cell.

As the king peered through the small glass window, he blinked his eyes and looked away and then looked again. His heart started pounding. The man that he saw sitting there could pass for his double when he was in his late teens. It was like looking at himself twenty-five years earlier. You can guess what was going through his mind. He was visibly shaken and he asked if he could enter the cell. The lieutenant responded that that particular inmate was the most violent they had ever had in the prison. He told the king they had to restrain him just to service the cell. He had attacked both officers and inmates since he had been incarcerated.

"He has no reason to live and nothing to lose," the lieutenant told him.

The king told him he could inform the warden if he had to, in order to get permission, but he wanted to go into the cell. The warden was informed, and it was decided they would shackle the inmate to the wall to allow the king to enter. He tried to convince the king to allow a couple of officers into the cell with him, but the king insisted on entering alone.

When the cell door slammed behind the king, he was met with a barrage of profanity and threats: "Who the _____ are you and what the _____ do you want? I will rip your _____ head off if you'll come over here." With that, the inmate spit on the king and immediately two large officers stormed into the cell to retaliate, saying; "that's the king, you _____." But the king held them back. They stood there momentarily with the inmate taunting them. It took all of their restraint to obey the king's command and they slowly and grudgingly backed away and returned to the corridor.

King Alanado took out his handkerchief and wiped himself off and then sat on a stool across the cell. The verbal abuse continued: "You're the _____ king of this _____ _____ _____ country. Did you come down here to get killed because I would be glad to _____ do it for you. What do you want? Did you come to see me die? Come over here and I'll take you with me." It continued like that for several minutes. The king just sat silently looking at the inmate. "What are you looking at you _____ _____ moron?"

The king endured the abuse until the inmate fell silent. He asked, "Where are you from and why did you come to

Sabothenia?" He could tell by his accent that he was a foreigner.

"None of your _____ business you _____ moron," was the reply.

"Who are your parents?"

"What the ____ do you care, _____."

What the king saw sitting before him was a deranged nineteen-year-old who probably had below a ninth-grade education. He was addicted to drugs, sex and violence, and he was full of bitterness, cynicism and hatred. After a couple more minutes without any satisfactory response, the king got up and left the cell.

The warden was waiting for him with the officers, all of them very disturbed at what their king had just endured. The king asked them to unshackle the inmate, but under no circumstances was he to be punished. He asked if they had a private room where he could be alone for a few minutes. The warden showed him to an empty office and left him there.

Alanado was overcome with emotion and wept. He was convinced that he had just seen and talked to his son. He knew it. There was no mistaking it. Nothing could have ever prepared him for the impact of the discovery. After several minutes, when he pulled himself together, he spoke to the warden and the officers in private. He told them that he believed De Honden was possibly his son. He also said the information must be kept under strict secrecy. They swore a solemn oath to their king that what they had seen and heard would not go beyond the room, not even to their families.

The king told them that there was a new process developed in England that had to do genes and chromosomes. It could prove beyond any doubt if two people were related or not. He was going to look into having the inmate and himself tested to find out if his suspicions were correct. Later that day the king would contact a trusted friend in the British government to make arrangements for the tests. No one involved would know who the two subjects were. A researcher would be sent to take the samples. At that time it could take a month or more before they would have an answer.

Shortly after leaving the prison that day, the king arrived at the Royal Mansion. He took this wife by the arm and led her up to their private chambers. He closed several doors behind them and sat her down. He started his story in cautious measured sentences. He told her now, he also believed their son was alive. He was convinced that the man on death row was Renaldo. The queen froze in silent astonishment for several seconds and then let out a low, mournful cry. She then began to sob, and the sobbing turned into hysterical laughter. Her husband held her, and she wept in his arms.

Then, in a complete change of emotion, she threw her head back and demanded, "Take me to him!"

"We can't do that, dear," the king replied. "No one can know about this until the tests are complete and we have confirmation." He hoped by that time they would know what to do. "My dear, you must realize he is a murderer. I talked to him, he's violent and deranged. If I am right, it will take a miracle to make him into our prince."

"He is already our prince," the queen corrected. "The challenge is going to be to get him to understand who he really is. When he understands that, then he will change naturally."

What agony settled in for them. Eighteen years of believing and seeking had been painful, but relatively calm. Suddenly their dream was on the verge of fulfillment, but there were impossible obstacles in the path. The man was convicted of murder. How would that be worked out? Was it right to let him off? How could they just bring him into their family? What about their daughters? Those were just some of the thoughts that raced through their minds. They struggled with how much they should say to their daughters. They decided it was prudent to keep silent.

The next weeks were the hardest of their lives since the kidnapping. Reverend Lorente was contacted and asked to come to the Royal Mansion. He had retired several years earlier but was still close to the royal family and was often consulted for his perspective.

When they shared the king's discovery with him, he asked, "Are you sure that's it's him?"

The king said that he was 90 percent sure that they had found their son. "The resemblance is uncanny. His voice, his posture, his eyes are all a match to me. It was like talking to myself." He explained that the DNA fingerprinting method would let them know for sure in the next few weeks.

Their pastor told them they needed to be very careful. "Do you remember that boy from the U.S. that came forward a few years back? You thought that he was your son, and then he was proven to be a fraud. I don't want to see the two of you get hurt again."

The king responded, "I never really believed that he was my son. It just didn't fit like this does. We will withhold our emotional commitment until it is a fact, and Pristina will not meet him until then, but I know this is it. Pristina has had all of the certainty in the past, but now I am certain."

"What about the fact that he is a convicted murderer?" the reverend asked.

"That has no real bearing on the issue of him being my son," the king replied. "It's a completely separate issue, and we have to deal with one thing at a time. If he is my son, then I will know how to deal with the other. I have to consider all of the facts. He is also a victim here, kidnapped at one year of age. That has to count for something. I need to know where he has been the last eighteen years. What kind of hell has he lived through that made him into what he is today?"

The reverend sighed and fell silent for a few seconds. He was stopped by the king's forthright stance. He stood up and paced the floor with his head bowed and his hands clasped behind his back. Alanado and Pristina exchanged glances and waited for his response. Finally, he told them he would be praying for them and that if they needed to talk, he was there for them. They never did speak about it again.

Five agonizing weeks later the results came back. It was only after repeating the test two times and duplicating the same results that the information was released to the king and queen. De Honden was Renaldo Portance, Crown Prince of Sabothenia.

Chapter 9
THE BEST LAID PLANS

When the DNA results came back, proving that De Honden was the lost prince, the facts of his past life were cloaked in mystery. The king knew only one thing, he was his son who had been violently abducted eighteen years earlier. On the basis of that knowledge alone, he granted the prince a pardon. Of course, all of it was done in secret and would be kept that way until the entire circumstances were understood. The king had the prince brought to the Royal Mansion where he was reunited with his mother for the first time since he was a baby.

They sat the perplexed, angry young man down and his parents sat opposite him staring at one another. Alanado began to inform him of the facts as Pristina sat with a tissue wiping at he eyes and nose as he spoke. The prince's first reaction was unbelief. He laughed it off, as if it were a joke, and then asked them what kind of cruel and unusual punishment they were trying to impose on him. They told him that it was no joke, and it was no punishment, but that it was the truth. He responded that he was not even from Sabothenia. "I was born in the Netherlands."

They explained he might have grown up in the Netherlands, but he was not born there, he was born in this very house on March 21, 1969. They brought out photographs of him as a baby and also photos of the king taken when he was nineteen years old and showed the prince the amazing resemblance. They brought out a scrapbook of news clippings of the kidnapping and explained as much as they knew about what had happened. Finally, they had the royal physician come in and explain what DNA testing was and how it worked. The young man was told there was absolutely no doubt he was Crown Prince Renaldo Portance, the firstborn child of King Alanado and Queen Pristina Portance and heir to the throne of the Royal Kingdom of Sabothenia.

The prince sat dazed, as the reality began to sink into his disturbed young mind. If you remember, the queen had said, "When he understands the truth, then he will change." But his immediate reaction did not quite conform to her prediction. After a few moments of silent, inner-emotional turmoil, the newfound prince looked at his mother and father and spoke bitterly in his Dutch accent.

"Look, I know who the _____ I am and I'm not ashamed of it. I would do it all over again if I could. The people who I have hurt got what they deserved. You telling me that I'm your son and I am the Crown Prince cannot change who the _____ I am. I have spent my whole life being hounded and pursued by _____ like you, and I would rather face my punishment than become what you represent to me."

When he said that, the two officers who had accompanied him stood to their feet at the ready. The king and queen sat with stunned expressions on their faces. They thought that if they merely told him the truth that he would see it and they would have their son back. How could they have been so naive? They felt like fools. Their feelings of hope and optimism that had been building over the past weeks had just been run aground on the jagged rocks of reality. When they regained their composure, they had the prince shown to the quarters which had been prepared for him. The two officers who had brought him from the prison would be staying at the Royal Mansion until issues were resolved and settled.

The king and queen went into seclusion for several hours to try and recover. Yet again, they clung to each other in desperation and drew strength from their unity. After much soul searching, their emotional reaction began to quell and they saw a direction. It was a risk, but they had to take it. They would give the prince the choice of returning to death row or staying in the Royal Mansion. They could not force their will upon him; they would have to give him his freedom. He had to choose his destiny. Since the public or the media did not know about the prince, they could return him to the prison if he so chose.

That evening they met with him again, and the king presented the options. The prince was proud, but he wasn't stupid. Once he had time to think about it, he swallowed some of his pride and chose to stay and live. He insinuated that he could ruin them with the knowledge that he had. But inside, his reasoning was, "I'll take advantage of whatever I can get."

He told them, "I accept that you are my parents, but keep your distance. You represent everything to me that I have resented all of my life. I hate who you are and what you stand for, and if I take advantage of you now, then I think that is real justice."

The king was not accustomed to or willing to be badgered, controlled or manipulated. He responded by making it very clear, in no uncertain terms, that the prince was a guest in their house, and he would be subject to and obey the rules if he wished to remain. The prince smirked and did not respond. He was testing the fences and learning the boundaries. He knew he had a very good thing and he was learning how far he could push. He was returned to his quarters and the king and queen returned to theirs. They were hurting almost more than when the kidnapping took place. The reality of what had happened to their child was overwhelming. Again, they held each other in desperation.

Over the next couple of days, an uneasy détente was reached. The servants at the mansion were told that there was a visitor who would be staying for awhile. They were not to ask questions about it or speak of it among themselves, or outside of the Royal Estate. The other children, Loraine and Julia, were staying with relatives the day that the prince arrived. They had been informed that their older brother had been found when the DNA results came back. They were very excited too, but their parents told them because of the condition they found the prince in, it would be better for them if they were away when he arrived. Their parents cautioned them that it was not going to be as easy as they had hoped. As a matter of fact, it would be better if they stayed with relatives for awhile until things settled down.

Alanado and Pristina looked at the facts. The closure they had sought and believed for still eluded them. They encouraged themselves that they were getting closer, however. As a matter of fact, they had taken a giant step forward. What were the odds of them ever finding the crown prince again? They were the only ones in the world who believed it possible. So, just as they had believed against all odds to find their son again, they would have to believe against all odds to see him change. Even if it looked impossible, their long-range goal was to prepare the prince to be the future ruler of the realm. Once their minds were clear and set, they would not be deterred. They began to make positive confessions about the future, even though the circumstances made it look impossible.

On the outside, the prince changed fairly rapidly. He had a multitude of servants to groom and manicure him. He was given fine clothes to wear and excellent food to eat. He had the best of medical and dental care. He began to look like a prince. And what a handsome one he was: six feet, three inches tall, with a muscular frame, dark, wavy hair with flashing green eyes, aristocratic nose and a dimpled square chin. Even though you might detest him, you could not dismiss the power of his personality when he chose to reveal his smile.

But the heart is where the issues are. He was trying to make contacts for drugs through the staff of the Royal Mansion. He manipulated, intimidated, threatened and tried to use his position to accomplish his goals. The entire staff had to be let in on who he was, informed of his personality traits, and warned to be cautious around him. The women were told to never be alone in his presence. The Royal Mansion, which had always been a place of stately calm, became a place of anxiety and tension. Also, the circle of those who were in the know about the prince was growing larger. It was imperative, at least at that point, that the secret be kept. The king and queen had the loyalty and respect of their people, but they didn't know how the pardon of the prince would be received. They pondered about how they might make the information public. They needed to buy as much time as they could, until they could figure out how to do it and get the prince prepared at the same time.

After the prince's first week at the mansion, the king and queen decided to bring their daughters home for a visit. They reasoned that it might have a positive effect on their son. The first meeting was rather awkward for all. Renaldo had to be escorted to the meeting by his officers. There he sat between them, very disinterested and seemingly bored.

Queen Pristina: "Renaldo, we want you to meet your sisters."

Loraine: "Hello, Renaldo. I'm Loraine; it's nice to meet you."

Julia: "Hi, Renaldo. I'm Julia, and I've been looking forward to meeting you."

Renaldo: "If what they say is true, I guess that you're right. You are my sisters."

Renaldo was acting indifferent, but he was not quite as arrogant and obnoxious as in the recent past. It was clear to the king and queen the meeting was worthwhile. Later, they reasoned that Renaldo had always distrusted adults and was able to identify with youth. After awhile the parents did withdraw to the other side of the room and allowed the girls to speak to him. There seemed to be some rapport and a relationship was developing. He asked them some things about their lives and confessed some things about his. Later Loraine's comments about her older brother were hopeful, but cautious. Julia said that she didn't think he was as bad a person as she had heard. She also wanted to know when they would be able to move back home. Her parents would not commit and only said that it would happen as soon as they determined it to be safe.

It was so hard for the king and queen because they loved Renaldo so much and he treated them so poorly. They patiently suffered through it. But even though they were vulnerable, they did not lose control of the situation. They remained confident that progress was being made even when they couldn't see it. Daily they made every attempt to express their love for him and show their desire to have a relationship. They could see some ice beginning to melt; at least they could converse with him. They continued to make positive steps toward their goal.

Renaldo needed an evaluation of his education, but they were not sure how to approach it. They had a friend who was an educator come and talk with him to get some idea where to start. It was very difficult for him to talk to Renaldo as Rendaldo was threatened by the subject of education and would not cooperate. From the conversation, the teacher could see that Renaldo was extremely intelligent, but guessed that academically he was going to require a lot of work. What he lacked most was a teachable attitude. Nothing could be done until that was in place.

It became a struggle for the prince to maintain his bad attitude in the face of the steady unconditional love of his parents. He was losing his identity as a rebel and that made him insecure. It was a war of wills. It was not in his genre to lose. He lay awake at night trying to cope with his dilemma. His evil mind did not let him down.

Chapter 10
THE FINAL TEST

With a mind that was accustomed to twisting and turning, the prince came up with a plan that he thought would show his parents up for who he thought they really were. Early one morning he placed some blankets in his bed to make it look like he was still sleeping. He slipped out a window and climbed down the wisteria and worked his way through the foliage to find a hiding place outside the kitchen. He was waiting for the grocery delivery truck that came in at six a.m. When it went out the gate that morning, he was hiding in the back. At the truck's next stop in the city, he was free.

He slipped back into the old neighborhood and found some of his acquaintances. The first thing he did was get loaded and set out to have some fun. He thought that it would finally resolve his emotional turmoil and dash the foolish aspirations of the king and queen. He would teach them to try and love him. About the time that the officers discovered that he was not in his bed, he was standing in a small market demanding money from the clerk.

As Renaldo left the store and rounded the corner into the parking lot, he ran into two policemen who immediately took him into custody. How ironic that was, considering all of the years that he ran wild. He tried to pull one small job and was immediately apprehended. The police took him in and he was charged. Of course they knew who he was and they were baffled as to how he got on the street. When they contacted the prison, Renaldo's father was notified by the warden. Within minutes, Alanado showed up at the local precinct with the prison officers and took the prince back to the Royal Mansion.

But the word was out. Certain people in the media had been wondering what was happening in the royal family. Why were the girls staying with their aunt? Who was the stranger at the Royal Mansion that one of the help had mistakenly mentioned? The picture was starting to come together. It was quickly becoming a feeding frenzy. The news spread across the country within hours.

I watched these events unfold. By then, I was anchorman for National Television, and my producer was insisting that I do an exposé. He said that I knew the royal family well, and no one would be more suited than I. Our station would be guaranteed worldwide coverage.

"If we don't move forward immediately, someone will scoop us," he told me.

I advised caution and tried to stall him. "We need more background and verification," I said. I refused to be pushed into it, even though it could have cost me my position.

The station interviewed the wife of the slain policeman on the 6:00 news. It was carried by affiliates around the world. People were first amazed and then outraged. The king and queen were harboring a cop killer at the Royal Mansion. What happened to justice in the nation? The king and queen believed him to be their lost son. DNA fingerprinting was hardly known at that time and most people did not understand that explanation, let alone accept it. They believed that the king and the queen had gone so far off the deep end that they took this foreign murderer in as their son. And the thought that he was next in line to be king was unthinkable. Their obsession to find their dead son was finally ruining the country. Members of the government themselves were very concerned and some threatened to resign. The next day, there were protests in

Capriel and a couple of other cities. Marchers were demanding the prince's execution. By the end of the week, people were rioting in several places in Sabothenia. How the rest of the world was eating it up; many received it with glee. All of their suspicions about "the perfect nation" were being confirmed as the truth was finally coming out.

So, the king and queen had a crisis on their hands, but, by then, they were used to standing against the grain. They had been doing it for the previous eighteen years. They were not about to throw away all that had been accomplished. They refused to let public opinion dictate right and wrong. They were in control and they would remain in control. They put the National Police and the army on alert and dispatched forces to check the rioting. At the time, they didn't know that what looked like a crisis was really an answer.

It was an answer because of the impact it had on the next ruler of the nation, the prince. He knew that his dad had pardoned him once, but when he had pardoned him a second time, that gave him pause. How could it be? It was not within the realm of his comprehension. His stronghold of bitterness, selfishness and anger was beginning to crumble. "After knowing me, he still pardoned me," he thought. "My parents care more about me than they do about their own lives or future. The public hates me, and they're right, I do deserve to die, but my parents won't allow it. They are willing to fight to save me and sacrifice their kingdom in the process."

On the fifth day after the crisis started, he came to his parents and asked them to let him go back to death row in order to resolve it. His parents just stood there stunned, in silent awe.

The prince continued, "I don't know why you even pardoned me the first time. I don't even get why you wanted to talk to me after you looked into my cell. Why have you subjected your family and the nation to me? You could have just kept your suspicions to yourself and then walked away and no one would have ever known."

When the king and queen heard that, they knew they truly had their son back. His father replied, "You are our son; we have searched for you and longed for you for years. We would take you back no matter what condition we found you in. The longer we were without you, the more intense our pain became. And now that we finally have you, no one will ever take you away from us again."

The prince broke into tears with his head in his hands. The king and queen gathered around him and placed their arms around him. The three of them just held each other and wept. The servants heard loud, mournful sobbing coming from the royal chambers.

From that point on the prince's eyes opened more each day. He began to see and appreciate who he really was. He was born in the likeness of his father into the royal household. He was entitled to all of the privileges that position brought. He was not a miserable dog begging to eat crumbs under the table. He was born with favor, dignity and destiny. He had been deceived into believing he was unworthy to receive anything of value. He believed the only way he would ever have anything was to steal it. He began to view his past with horror and regret. It angered him that he had been so deceived and so much had been stolen from him. He began see himself as the prince he truly was.

Within a couple of days Loraine and Julia came home. There was laughter and teasing and joy in the Royal Mansion to a degree which had never happened before. There was life in the house that had been missing for eighteen years. A new family dynamic was developing. The servants were also experiencing this breath of fresh air. It was a time of great rejoicing. It had been so tense for so long that the contrast was remarkable, so remarkable that the news media heard about it. It was so incongruent with what they expected was happening there, hardly any of them believed it to be true. I understood what was happening because of my familiarity with the royal family. I rejoiced with them.

The girls were so excited to have the older brother who had only been a fantasy in the past. But what a collision of values; at times it was very awkward for all. The prince's lack of education and cultivation was obvious. The prince was constantly humbled by his own words and behavior. His younger sisters had to understand that there were deep scars and habits which would only be healed and changed with time. He was constantly plagued by guilt and self-degradation for the things that he had done. When he was down he received encouragement and support from his family. Many in the public hated him and wished him dead, but he had a family who believed in him and supported every positive move he made. Renaldo depended on their help each day and they, in return, witnessed beauty emerge from desolation.

The prince asked that a meeting be arranged with the slain police officer's family. It was very difficult for both parties involved. In tears and anguish he confessed his crime before them and pleaded for their forgiveness. The family was reluctant to even come to the meeting, let alone forgive him. They vented their pain and anger upon the prince, but when they saw the depth of his humility and remorse, they softened. The one exception was Celeste, the slain policeman's daughter. She claimed that she could never forgive him for what he had done. She said that the prince had taken something from her that could never be replaced and as far as she was concerned, he could go to hell. The prince said that he understood and sadly accepted her decision. Though it was not the complete healing that was needed, it was a major step in the process for both families. There were some things the prince knew he would have to live with and would never be forgotten. Day by day and week by week, his life changed. He began to take on the image of his father. He already looked like him, but he had begun to act like him.

When the public began to understand that De Honden really was the lost prince, it partially quelled the fervor of their outrage. That left the issue of the murder to deal with. The prince was a murderer. Is it just to set a murderer free? How did the royal family justify that action? The king knew he had to address the issue. He had followed his heart in pardoning the prince. He did not fully understand if his action was just in the legal sense of the word. In light of the circumstances at that time, he and the queen felt that it was the right thing to do. They could not allow his death sentence to be carried out.

In hindsight, the king had begun to wonder if he had been too hasty and should have handled the death sentence differently. If all the facts were known at the prince's trial, would it have made a difference? But what were the facts? How did the prince become a gangster, committing the horrible crimes that he committed? The royal legal counsel told them that the prince was guilty of murder, but that he could have gotten a reduced or suspended sentence if all the facts had been known. Some in return argued that any crime could be justified on those grounds and that many people could use their past to declare their innocence. They said that anyone could claim special circumstances in their life that could be grounds for acquittal. Should the prince be held accountable for his crime? The question hung over the nation like an unexploded bomb awaiting detonation.

Chapter 11
THE CONFESSION

In a darkened room a solitary figure lay flat on his back in constant agony. Any normal human who viewed the forsaken soul would react with revulsion first, and then with horror at the hand that misfortune had dealt. How could a loving God allow that kind of death to befall any of His creatures? It might be a mystery to many and cause their faith to be forfeited in a sea of uncertainty, but not to the one who knew the truth behind the tragedy.

In this particular case, the only person who knew the truth was the victim himself. He had begun to suspect that his condition was the result of his life of debauchery and evil. In years past, he'd had utter distain for the "morally righteous," but since that time he had come to see that there are consequences in life, consequences from which not even money and power can grant immunity. Since that realization, fear and dread had been his constant companions as he lay there waiting to die.

The door opened a crack to reveal a blinding shaft of light. A voice broke the monotonous silence. "Mr. Poscatal, can I come in?" It was the facility chaplain who had been trying to develop rapport with the patient for some time. As of late, there had been a breakthrough of sorts; Mr. Poscatal had begun to confer with the chaplain. It was nothing too serious, a mere exchange of pleasantries and a venting on the unfairness of life. But it was an opening for the chaplain to perhaps minister to this miserable soul.

That day he shared the latest headline with the patient. "Sir, have you heard that they think that they have found the lost prince?" There was an awkward silence as the patient became absolutely still and stopped breathing momentarily.

After a few seconds a weak voice responded, "What did you say?"

The chaplain repeated, "The lost prince, they think that they have found the lost prince."

Of course, reports about the lost prince were nothing new; he had been spotted and found numerous times over the years. But they invariably turned out to be hoaxes or overactive imaginations.

The chaplain went on to explain, "This is not the typical prince sighting, it has apparently been verified by a new scientific means using genetic information that has proven it to be for certain. This news actually has come out of Sabothenia. Imagine, after all of these years, the prince being found."

Poscatal lay motionless and stunned. How could that have happened after all of his maniacal maneuvering to destroy the prince's life? It could happen only by some unknown force; a force beyond that discernable by normal means; the same force that he would answer to in the very near future. The news positioned Poscatal at an emotional tipping point.

The next day, as the chaplain was making his usual rounds, Poscatal told him that he had a special request. He wanted to make a confession and he asked the chaplain to invite someone from the law enforcement community to his room to receive it. One condition he required was that his revelations not be released until his death. The Brussels Police Department, who took the confession, analyzed it and deemed it credible. A criminal prosecution was in order but there was no point; Poscatal was very close to death. He died within the week and a transcript was passed on to the proper authorities in Sabothenia.

After the king and queen read it and partially recovered from the initial impact, they asked me to come to the Royal Mansion as quickly as possible. When I arrived, they handed it to me. They sat, the queen weeping silently, and watched me as I read. When I was finished, and my eyes met theirs, all three of us gazed at each other in silent astonishment. We were incredulous.

I asked the king, "Your Majesty, can I release this to the media?"

King Alanado replied to me, "I think that it needs to be made public, don't you?"

I shook my head in agreement.

It hit the newsstands the following morning in Sabothenia, and that night evening news broadcasts carried it around the world. The transcript was as follows:

> My name is Lieutenant Hans Gilsoul of the Brussels Police Department. On July 18, 1988, I was accompanied by my fellow officer, Sergeant Mikhail Tourgonin, to hear a confession of a Mr. Durando Poscatal at the Evinrudde Care Center. Mr. Poscatal had requested our presence to hear his confession on the condition that its contents not be made public until after his death. Our department agreed to that request only on the grounds that no life would be endangered by information being withheld. Also present in the room was the facility chaplain, Mr. Rolf Devries, and a department stenographer. The content of Mr. Poscatal's statement is as follows:

"My name is Durando Poscatal and being of sound mind I do hereby make this statement in the presence of witnesses. I was formerly Lord Durando Poscatal, Administrator of the Budget of the Royal Kingdom of Sabothenia. I was relieved of my position by King Alanado Portance in 1968 for "a lack of integrity" in the performance of my official duties. I was indeed guilty of receiving kickbacks from key contractors to whom I awarded prime public works projects. I had amassed a substantial fortune over the years and upon my dismissal I went into exile and eventually settled in Brussels, Belgium.

"I was furious at having been exposed and removed from office, and the desire for revenge consumed me. Because of a security audit that I had performed on the Royal Estate, I knew of a flaw in the system which would allow me access to the compound. I had the security evaluation done in 1966 in the hope that I might be able to retrieve evidence against me compiled by King Marsalis. He died and I thought that my problem had died with him, but his son found certain documents and that is when he acted against me. At first, I thought of nothing but doing harm to the king, and I knew that with the information that I had, I could slip into the mansion and carry it out. But, as time passed, another thought occurred to me and because of my deranged condition it appealed to me even more. It was the day the world celebrated the birth of the prince that the evil scheme entered my mind. My plan was to take the thing the world and the king and queen cherished the most, and destroy it— the new prince. That undertaking has been the ruin of my life and many other lives. It has led me to commit unimaginable crimes and ultimately resulted in this horrible disease from which I am soon to die.

"A man named Longo Natras, who ran a security consulting firm in Capriel, was the only other person who knew about the security flaw. I threatened him and forced him out of the country before I was removed from office. I kept tabs on him after that because he was the only weak link in my scheme. As long as he was quiet and stayed out of Sabothenia, I told him he would remain alive. He also settled in Brussels, and I gave him subsistence from time to time. I meticulously planned the abduction of the prince and carried it out flawlessly. I had the money, the time, the physical strength and the desire to make it work. It was a challenge that gave me a reason to live until it was accomplished. It was I who was hiding in the bushes that morning when the governess came by with the prince. I came up behind her and placed a rag containing halothane over her face until she was unconscious. I removed the prince from his stroller and held him under my arm. I left nothing behind that could be traced or give a clue. I went out as I came in, over the wall with a rope ladder which I also removed and took with me. My vehicle was hidden a short way from the estate and I was seen by no one. I was probably out of the country before the first police arrived at the scene.

"I went immediately to a prearranged location in the Netherlands and there I stayed with the child until the searching had subsided. I took care of him for two months in absolute secrecy. I had already researched an underworld family who lived in Amsterdam. They trafficked in human beings. Mostly for prostitution, but I had heard from sources that they occasionally purchased children for use in pornography and other criminal activities. When the time was right, I approached them with the offer of a baby. They never knew who the child was that they purchased. He was such a bright and healthy child, they were beside themselves to get their hands on him. For me, it was the height of revenge to let the child live and suffer in a situation that I knew would be a world of darkness and depravity. I deserve a thousand deaths far worse than what I am suffering now for what I did. I only hope that God will have mercy on me because of this confession.

"For the next few years, I kept tabs on the prince to ensure that all was going as planned. I had a regular liaison with a young lady who belonged to his family. She kept me informed as to what kind of misery and evil was befalling my worst enemy's son. At that time in my life, I had no remorse; quite to the contrary, I reveled in his hardship and received satisfaction from her dismal reports. He was regarded much like an animal being raised for slaughter: fed, but never named. He was just an investment that needed to be maintained. Therefore, he received the necessities to sustain life, but was never touched or shown affection. When any family member started to show emotion or signs of familiarity with him, they were disciplined for it. Much of the time he was locked in a room. If he misbehaved, he was beaten. Eventually, he came to be known as *De Honden*, or "the dog." That was the only name that he ever received from them. As he grew older the abuse continued.

"It was amazing and uncanny how well he endured and survived his torment. Though he was a prisoner, he held power over his captors. There was always something about him that they could not understand and his spirit could not be broken. Now I know that it was favor that surrounded him and protected him. Favor of a supernatural origin. Several times he escaped from them, but he was recaptured. At the age of eleven, he escaped for good. He knew that he was relatively safe on the street; they could not go to the authorities. That is where his owners and I lost contact with him. They searched for him, but were not able to find him and eventually they gave up. He disappeared into the underworld of Amsterdam. At that time, I was satisfied that my purpose had been achieved.

"My only concern through all of this was keeping Natras quiet. When Victor Swortha started poking around and found Natras, I knew that I had to act. I killed Natras and dumped his body in the canal. I searched his apartment for anything that could link me to him, but found nothing. Apparently Swortha did find something because he came back to Brussels looking for me. I was prepared for him. He thought that he was invincible but he played right into my hands. What was another murder at that point? I made sure that no one would ever find his body.

"Up to that time I had taken no life, but after the murders, my life grew darker and darker. I could find no pleasure in any worldly thing. I was tormented constantly by guilt, but deep-seated unforgiveness constantly helped me to justify my revenge. The constant pressure was more than my body could take, and my health started to decline and brought me to the state that I am in now. My hope is that by this confession I can somehow assuage the one that soon will judge my soul. Though I deserve no consideration for the things that I have done, at least I have done one thing right in this long and miserable life." Signed Durando Poscatal.

Chapter 12
PAINFUL PIECES

When the prince heard Poscatal's confession, he was overwhelmed with sorrow, resentment and anger. Another painful piece of the puzzle of his life was in place. But though the pieces were painful, they began to make a whole. He filled in the rest in the long conversations with his sisters. I was asked by Queen Pristina to chronicle all of the details. She reasoned that someday the complete truth could be made known, and she believed that I would tell it accurately.

After the boy's escape from his evil family, he learned how to live on the streets. Lying, cheating, stealing, sex, drugs and violence became a way of life for him. There were other urchins who lived in the underground of Amsterdam. He met a young girl a couple of years older than himself named Mia. They were attracted to each other and Mia became the first person that De Honden could remember caring about. They survived together and learned about life together. De Honden finally had the family he had been deprived of. This family was a loosely organized group of homeless castoffs. Being the natural leader that he was, his friends, even older ones, began to look to him for direction. He looked a couple of years older than his actual age, and he was handsome and muscular with a boldness and confidence that led others to trust him. In spite of his lack of education, he was articulate. He eventually became the leader of their community. Mia reigned with him. They became the Prince and Princess of Thieves. Several times De Honden was captured and placed in a youth facility. That was the only time he received any proper care or education. From the detention center he would go to foster care. From there he would escape back to the street and his real family of street gangsters. This cycle repeated itself numerous times over the years. The authorities finally labeled him as incorrigible and began to look the other way.

There were several policemen who did not look the other way. They hated dealing with De Honden and being humiliated by him. They believed he and his friends were being coddled by social services and never held accountable for their crimes. His fame grew even more as the result of several articles in the papers which glamorized his life and further humiliated the police. At that point, they made a pact to get rid of him by any means, and to cover for each other if there was a consequence. One night Mia was missing from their usual gathering. Though De Honden and his friends scoured the city for her, no one could find her. He was desperate. He was missing the only person that he'd ever cared about. It grew far worse for him when her body was found four days later. She had been murdered and there was no doubt in any of their minds who had done it. It is difficult for another person to describe the emotions that consumed De Honden. His despondency led to a careless attitude and behavior.

One night soon after Mia's murder, he was cornered by four officers with weapons drawn. "Oh, look what we have," one said. "I think that it's a little dog," said another. "Come with us little doggie, we have a treat for you." "We want to take you to see your girlfriend." They took him on his last ride to a wasteland outside the city. They opened the car door and pushed him out. One of the policemen raised his weapon to the prince's head and pulled the trigger. The gun misfired! The prince darted into the night, miraculously avoiding a hail of gunfire. He escaped unharmed.

He knew that he had to escape Holland, but where to go? Why not to the place that everyone believed to be safe, Sabothenia? There are events in this world that are far beyond coincidence:

a gun misfiring at the crucial time, a prince returning to the very place where he came from. Destiny is fulfilled most often unbeknownst to those who are destined.

The prince found the people of Sabothenia to be extremely naive. It was not at all like the streets of Amsterdam. The street life there was unsophisticated and backward in his estimation. The young people that he met needed to be taught what crime was. They thought that shoplifting from the department store was crime. He knew what the country needed. It needed someone to show the amateurs what real life was.

On the other hand, it was an extremely kind place. He was used to being chased out of public places and hunted by the authorities. In Sabothenia, there were people who wanted to help him. They wanted to give him a home or food. He was invited home by an elderly woman. When he first got to Capriel, she saw him wandering the streets and she offered him a place to stay. He went with her. He ate her food. He wore clothes that she gave him. He slept on her bed. And then he stole her jewelry. It was beyond his ability to resist, and what a haul it was. Once he had it, what could he do with it? After two days of searching he found an older foreigner who took it off his hands. As time went on he started to make contacts with a well hidden criminal element. He also hooked up with young people who were looking for someone to lead them.

With his contacts out of the country, he became a conduit for importing contraband into Sabothenia. Over the next few years he brought life into this "backward" nation with a good supply of drugs and weapons. The teenage girls in Sabothenia were hardly a challenge for him. With his good looks and smooth tongue, he took what he wanted. He cared about no one. His heart was hardened and he hated anything that stood for authority, tradition or established order, especially government. His life came to revolve around sex, drugs and violent crime, such as muggings and armed robbery. He directed a small army of young criminals and became a kingpin of organized teenage violence. Many came forward to carry out his wishes for him. Rivalries developed amongst the young criminals in their desire for recognition. Gang warfare erupted. A government agency created a taskforce to study the problem, but the son of Victor Swortha knew how to handle it.

Eduardo Swortha took personal charge and set out to eliminate the undesirable elements in Capriel. Because of police efforts it became more and more difficult for the young criminals to operate. Swortha, like his father was unrelenting. He had heard of De Honden and set traps for him and his followers. Likely places to be robbed were staked out. Decoys were used in notorious mugging locations. The heat was on for them and what used to be easy pickings was now risky. Several teens were arrested and they were getting closer to the leader. De Honden took the offensive and began a personal crime spree with the intention of fighting back against law enforcement's efforts.

They set fires as a distraction in order to carry out crimes. It was all-out warfare on the streets. One night De Honden was cornered by the police, but unlike before, he was armed and very determined not to repeat what happened in Amsterdam. A policeman approached him with weapon drawn to take him into custody. The officer lowered his weapon and said, "Put down your gun, son, I don't want to hurt you." De Honden, reliving his past experience, fired one shot through the policeman's heart. He escaped that night, but was caught in an all-out police manhunt several days later and arrested. He was tried, convicted and sentenced to death. He was sitting on death row waiting for his sentence to be carried out when the king made his fateful visit.

After Poscatal's confession and other details of the prince's life were made public, there was a tremendous outpouring of sympathy for him and the royal family. When the people saw the whole picture, there was a national mood swing in favor of the king's decision to pardon his son. Of course, there were some who would never forgive the prince and always believed he should have paid the ultimate price, but for the most part, people understood and accepted it. That was accelerated by the changes in his life. He came to exemplify the poise, dominion and majesty of a royal monarch. At the same, time he was noted for his compassion for the hurting, the oppressed and the downtrodden. He could identify with the person on the street and the prison inmate, and he tried to help them. Eventually, the public noticed, and forgave.

Chapter 13
THE CORONATION

It was a day like none other in Sabothenia. There was bustling activity. Before sunrise, preparations were being checked and rechecked. Families were preparing their finest clothing and children were being inspected from head to toe for cleanliness. The six matched horses that would pull the royal carriage were also being inspected and groomed. The hotels were filled with foreign dignitaries and media people. It was the day of the coronation.

By midmorning the Royal Palace was bedecked with flowers, flags and other ceremonial ornamentation befitting the occasion. By early afternoon Knights of the Realm were standing at attention with armor and weaponry ablaze in the brilliant sunlight. The parade route was lined with thousands of loyal citizens of the nation and thousands of others who came from all over the world to watch the historic event. They cheered and rejoiced as the procession of open carriages, cavalry, and foot soldiers slowly proceeded. Each carriage stopped to unload royalty at the red carpet leading into the grand hall of the Royal Palace. The last carriage in the procession was surrounded by the Elite Palace Guard who were arrayed in black and gold armor. Riding in the carriage was Prince Renaldo Portance and his beautiful wife, soon to be King Renaldo and Queen Celeste of the Royal Kingdom of Sabothenia. The spectacle, which was beyond description, was only diminished in regality and magnitude by the story behind it; a story that became another heralded tale in the rich and glorious history of the nation of Sabothenia.

The following day, I sat in my home awaiting a visitor. An acquaintance from the United States was in the country for the coronation and we had made arrangements to meet for lunch. Wesley Peeks was a fairly well known writer who had done several short pieces on Prince Renaldo over the years for the *Times* and other publications. In those efforts he had used me as a primary source and we had developed a cordial relationship as a result. Peek's most recent book on Jimmy Hoffa did not fair well; the critics were polite, but unenthusiastic. In the book he had explored unsubstantiated theories on the disappearance without any real resolution, and people were tired of hearing yet another Hoffa murder theory.

Peeks also had a secret habit; he enjoyed occasional trips to Las Vegas and, consequentially, was running in the red. He had been depending on the Hoffa book to shore up his personal economy. Because of its disappointing debut, he was desperate for a new subject. He wanted to do a book on Prince Renaldo, but he knew he didn't have the background necessary to do it justice. There had already been one disappointing attempt by an author trying to cash in on the subject. He believed there was only one person who could do the subject justice. In his mental processing he came up with an inspiration. Because of his personal relationship with me, he thought perhaps he could negotiate an agent's fee if he could get me signed to a book contract. He queried his publisher, Warren Tuskin, of Dunnaway House LLC and pitched the idea to him. Immediately, Tuskin responded with enthusiasm and Peeks was able to finagle a pretty sweet deal. Shortly after, he contacted me on another matter and casually brought up the possibility of a book. After several months of correspondence, we agreed on the meeting that was about to take place.

There was a knock and I opened the door and greeted Peeks with an extended hand and a welcoming smile.

"Wesley, so good to see you," I said, and we shook hands. I led him over tiled floors to the partially shaded patio in the center of the house. A table had been set for us. After we readjusted the chairs slightly to avoid the direct sunlight, we reclined and continued in casual conversation until the maid appeared to fill water glasses.

"Would you be ready for bread and salad, sir?"

"That would be fine, Salina," I told her.

Some wrens chirped in the background and Wesley appeared to be relaxed and comfortable. But then, in typical American fashion, he abruptly sprang into action and got right to the point.

"Saun, you know that Dunnaway is very interested in signing you for the book that we have discussed. They have asked me if I could get a preliminary sketch or outline from you."

"Well, I have volumes of material that needs to be condensed, Wesley, and I do have a pretty good idea of what direction it will go." I hesitated and added, "I'm just not sure if they'll like my ideas."

"What could there possibly be not to like?" Peeks countered. "They have seen your other work and fell all over themselves about it."

"Well, you must understand, Wesley, that I have been close to the royal family since the beginning of this affair, and now their perspective is my perspective. Because of that, I see some things in this whole story which are way beyond what most people have considered."

"What could that possible be?" he inquired with a nervous laugh. He was obviously not willing to accept any obstacles to his premeditated agenda.

"For lack of a better phrase, it's the *eternal perspective*," I told him.

"*Eternal perspective*? Elaborate," he said with another nervous laugh, but the look in his eyes said, "What in the ___ are you talking about?"

Resisting his intended intimidation, I calmly explained, "Well, King Alanado and Queen Pristina always believed contrary to the rest of the world about finding the prince, and in a nutshell, their belief had an influence on the end result…In other words, had they not had the perspective that they did, you would never have seen the coronation that you saw yesterday. It was their belief that produced that result."

"What?" Peeks said with a furrow in his brow. Then, half mocking, he asked, "Are you saying that what they believed had an influence on the physical outcome?"

When I let his question hang midair for a few seconds, he shifted to a more paternal tone, as if trying to guide me back in the direction of sanity. "Don't you really think that what they suspected all along just turned out to be right?"

"Absolutely not! It turned out the way it did because of what they believed." I was a little irritated by his direction. I had heard the same thing over and over before regarding the king and queen's stand of faith. "Had they not maintained their belief over the years, it would never have happened."

"Well, that is an interesting perspective," he said, retreating. Then, trying to refocus the conversation, he said calmly in the paternal tone, "But does this distinction have any real impact on the story of the prince?"

"It's really the best part of the story," I told him. "Can you see that if what I am saying is true, everyone needs to know about it? To overlook it would be like saving the oyster and tossing the pearl."

"I don't really see the significance, Saun; it sounds like you might be editorializing on historic fact." Peeks hated talking about anything that was remotely spiritual. It made him very uncomfortable. He was at a loss to even comment because it took him completely out of his element. He really didn't know what to say other than to dissuade me from it. But as I went on, occasionally he nodded as if it was the most natural thing in the world for him to be sitting in a patio garden talking about faith in God.

I tried explaining it to him in as simple terms as I could. "Perhaps you've heard the saying, 'when you pray, believe that you have the things that you ask for and you will receive them.' In our way of thinking, it makes more sense to say 'when you pray, *receive* the things that you ask for and then you will *believe* them.' That would be easy, but that's not how it works. The believing has to come before the receiving. Do you see what I'm saying, Wesley? It's a supernatural principle of faith. If what I'm saying is true, don't you think that it would be a good idea to let people know about it? It was by this same supernatural principle that the prince was returned to his parents. They believed and prayed in spite of the circumstances for as long as it took, and they got what they believed for."

He remained silent, but there were three furrows in his brow by then. He saw his well-thought-out scheme being derailed. He was beginning to make a comment when Salina appeared again and placed some warm bread and salad on the table. As he confessed to me later, he was wondering if he had gotten himself into a Nostradamus controversy or something of that nature. He was wondering why couldn't I just tell the "damn" story without all of that.

After Salina left again, some irritation slipped out and he quipped sarcastically, "It sounds like you want to write a religious book to me, Saun." He instantly regretted his comment.

"Call it what you like, Wesley, but if you want the whole story on the prince, you have to look at the whole picture. Let's face it, you and I along with the rest of the world did not give the king and queen a snowball's chance in Hades of ever seeing their son again. For years, they were the butt of jokes for the stance that they took. And then when the impossible happened, and the prince turned up, you along with everyone else brushed it off as a mere coincidence. It's time to face the truth on the subject, as unpleasant as it may be; there is much more here than meets the eye. The only question is, can you handle it?"

I could read his thoughts in response; it was the first passion that he had ever seen in me; I had always been noted for my amiability. I had shocked him. He thought that I would roll over as an easy sell and he never anticipated any bumps. I decided right then that I might as well get it all out because he was going to hear about it sooner or later anyway.

"You might as well know Wesley, the story of the prince is more than a biographical human interest piece about a prince in a fairytale kingdom. And it's even more than the fact that the king and queen received their son back through their faith. The story of the prince is the story of your life and the life of almost every person that has ever been born on this planet!"

He was almost flabbergasted by that. I could see twinges of fear in his eyes. He had known me on a professional level for quite some time and had never heard me say anything so outlandish. His frustration was drifting into embarrassment for me and he was beginning to twitch in his patio chair. Realistically, from his worldly perspective, I was beginning to look like I was nuts. I knew he was desperate for a way to refocus the conversation, but there was a lot of money at stake for him and he didn't want to mess it up. I think that he resolved at that point to ride out the storm and hope for the best.

You see, I had figured it out from the beginning that Peeks was motivated purely by financial gain. But I had no intention of writing the book solely for profit. I was determined to take advantage of the opportunity to see that the truth was finally made known. My sense of justice demanded it. If for no other reason than I had watched the king and queen endure humiliation for years. I truly believed that it was my turn to bring some balance. The world was about to taste my wrath, but at the same time, they might hear something that they needed to know. I had liked Wesley and had enjoyed talking to him since we'd met, but right then I didn't mind rubbing his nose in truth for a few minutes. God knows he needed to hear it.

"De Honden thought that he knew who he was and he was deceived for the first part of his life. Do you think that his wrong thinking could change the fact of who he really was? What if the king had looked into that death row cell, recognized his son, but then turned and walked away and never said a word? The sentence would have been carried out and the prisoner would have received the punishment that he deserved. But they would have put the Crown Prince to death! Our ignorance of truth can not alter reality. But how many people pass through this world in the same ignorance? That is the greatest tragedy of the entire human drama: like the prince, people not knowing who they really are and what their lives should or could have been, having been deceived by some false reality that has robbed them of their true identity, purpose and destiny.

We both sat back in our chairs as Salina silently cleared away the salad dishes. Perspiration was appearing on Peek's forehead and he was starting to look a little sick. He had to be wondering where it was going to end. I think that he saw thousand dollar bills flying out the window. I didn't know it then, but he also thought that someone had told me about the problems he was going through.

Salina served the main course of roast lamb, steamed red potatoes and grilled asparagus, but at that point Peeks had pretty much lost his appetite. After she left, I went on.

"How old are you Wesley, fifty-five? Have you ever wondered about any of this before?"

"Well sure, Saun, all the time," he lied.

"The fact is, my friend, the truth is far more dignified than you could have ever imagined. It is by no means any less amazing than the story of the prince. Consider this: just as the prince resembled his dad, you were fashioned in the image of the one who made you. And you were born with destiny and purpose on your life. You were intended to have dominion on the earth. That's more than just being head of the food chain. It means that you are the Creator's very best; his crowning achievement, created in his likeness. If this is *not* your understanding, then *you* are the one that has been kidnapped, Wesley. Kidnapped, raised in deception and blinded to the truth of who you *really* are." His mouth hung opened slightly. He resembled a patient in a surgeon's office receiving the brunt of his preoperational analysis. He didn't comprehend if the news was good or bad, or how painful or costly it was going to be to get it fixed.

"But you know, Wesley, like the prince, you are being pursued by someone who has never given up hope of finding you and getting you back. There is no replacement for you. There is no one like you even if you were an identical twin. No one can do what you were created to do. No one can take the position that was prepared for you to fill and if you don't fulfill it, it will remain vacant for eternity. It's a place in the king's heart that is empty without you. It hurts. He can't ignore it, and he won't give up until he has the son back that has been stolen from him."

Ah, there it was. For the first time, Peaks was moved emotionally in a positive way. I had finally struck a chord. The words sliced through his armor and hit a vital spot. He didn't really comprehend what it was I said that touched him, but a dam had broken inside of him; and emotions he had not felt for years began spilling out. He fought them back and I moved in for the kill.

"He wept when he found you on death row waiting to pay the price for your crimes. You deserved the punishment that was planned for you. But he looked beyond the crime and recognized you as his lost son. In a single act of mercy, he pardoned you unconditionally. He brought you into his very presence. He saw your flaws and still loved you. He saw beyond your appearance and recognized the prince that you were always destined to be. He wants to love you into who you really are. He's willing to risk the embarrassment and liabilities that may come to him until you become that person. His ears are deaf to your accusers who are contending for your execution. You are a thing of beauty to him. He is rejoicing to have you back in any condition. And what can you do to deserve this honor? Nothing; he loves you because you breathe."

The hardened, middle-aged man was embarrassed by the tears welling up in his eyes and rolling down his cheeks. He had been touched in a way that he was completely unprepared for. He picked up his napkin wiped them away and tried to cover up the emotion. He'd believed in God as a child, but he hadn't thought about Him for years and he had never heard Him explained in such a personal way before. After the turmoil he had been through in preceding months, he was hearing just what he needed to hear.

I was aware of his embarrassment and out of courtesy I looked the other way. "We are not miserable sinners scrounging to get into the king's presence, Wesley, we were formed there and it was always his will for us to remain there. Unfortunately, we were deceived like the prince and the king has moved in our favor to restore us. Somewhere in your future, Wesley, if you begin to recognize who you really are, and if you listen very hard, you will hear great laughter and rejoicing. Can you hear it? It is a mighty multitude in celebration. It is a coronation beyond any that has ever taken place on this earth. The sons and daughters of the king are gathered in a place that is more spectacular than the world's greatest cathedral. Their armor is shining brighter than any sun could make it shine. You are meant to be there with them, Wesley. Standing in their midst in the rightful place that you were destined to fill for all eternity. Evil forces have tried to prevent the day, but they will have fallen and the pain of your suffering will have been forgotten. The time of celebration will have come and you will be waiting for the real guest of honor to arrive. He is the one who rescued you from death row. You are the joy that was set before him and made his suffering worthwhile. You are the prize that he is coming to receive and you can rejoice with him for all eternity."

Peeks' jaw was in a lowered position and he was looking directly at me, but not seeing me. He was looking through me into a distant past. His mind was playing a video of a relationship that had been forgotten and abandoned so long ago. It had the feel of a warm summer day with butterflies flitting about the garden and birds chirping from the trees. All the feelings that his thoughts produced way back then were coming forth. And he could clearly see that it was the things that he pursued in life that brought an end to what he once had. And to think that he gave it up for something that held the promise of glory, but produced only emptiness. It was a sobering realization, but at the same time, it restored him.

I fell silent and let him soak it in. Salina came to retrieve our dishes and asked, "Coffee?" "Yes" I told her. She looked over and could see that something had happened to Wesley, but she maintained her professional poise and poured the coffee. After drinking a cup, we said goodbye and Peeks left. He never did comment directly on what happened to him that day, but he walked out with a sobriety and peace he had not known since childhood. I think that he finally understood what I meant when I said the "*eternal perspective*" because he never argued with me about it again. As a matter of fact, later he insisted that I include the substance of our conversation in the book. I retired to my study, booted my computer and began to write.

And so there you have it; it was I, Saun Hoffmann, who made the full story of the prince known to the world. As I said at the beginning, there is meaning, destiny and purpose in the universe. I had been placed in a unique position to observe and understand the events as they unfolded. I was given favor with the royal family to become the prince's biographer for the first half of his life. I wrote the all-time bestseller which was published by Dunnaway House LLC. For me it was the culmination of a lifelong desire to write and leave something of lasting value to the world. When it was complete, I was satisfied that the main purpose of my life had been fulfilled. But the truth is, the most important story, the reign of Prince Renaldo was just beginning, and how I wished that I could be its teller. But that destiny was not for me. I had to leave it for another at future time.

CONTINUED…

QUESTIONS: Did this book speak to you? Is it worth sharing with someone else? If that answer to those questions is yes, then please pass it on.

Thanks, the Author

THE PORTANCE DYNASTY

Book two: THE RISING STAR

Book three: DARKNESS TO LIGHT

Other books by BRUCE EDWARD BUTLER

ALOUDA

THE IMMIGRANT

Purchase books and contact the author at

bruceedwardbutler.com

ABOUT THE AUTHOR

Bruce Butler started his writing career as a singer/songwriter in the early 1970s. In the '80s and early '90s he played in two bands and wrote many of the songs that they performed and recorded.

In 1993 he was asked by a friend to lead worship at an Oregon state prison. Soon, he was writing messages and preaching in Oregon and Washington prisons on a regular basis. In 1997 he became a volunteer jail chaplain, which he continues to do. He also does chapel services for Teen Challenge USA.

Much of his fiction has evolved from parables and metaphors used in messages to make deeper realities understandable. His first novel, *The Portance Dynasty* was copyrighted in 2007 and *Alouda* in 2009. Over the years, his method and medium have changed, but his purpose has never changed; it has always been to liberate and encourage people with God's goodness as revealed by his Word.

He and his wife, Karin, have eight children and ten grandchildren and live happily in Happy Valley, Oregon.

Made in the USA
Charleston, SC
30 August 2010